# ORCA RISING

## CHRIS HANNON

# ORCA RISING

# 1

# TESTS

'This summer will shape and define the course of the rest of your lives.'

Ocean yawned. How many times had he heard *that* in the last month? The lecture theatre was crammed with his year group and he was surprised to see the seriousness and fear on their faces. What was everyone getting so het up about? They were only GCSEs.

Mr Draper, the headmaster, went on: 'Whatever the outcome of your exams, it will propel you all in many different directions. Some may leave and enter the world of work, others may decide to stay on and do their A-Levels. All I will say is this,' his hands clasped like a politician, 'you have a chance now to build a platform for later years. Seize it! I implore you! The world needs fine young minds to shape it for the better.'

The staff clapped first, triggering the rest of the lecture theatre to beat their hands together or thump palms onto wooden desks. Ocean saw this "special assembly" for what it was—a cheap trick to scare the lazier ones among them to revise harder. Some idiot whooped.

Ocean didn't clap. Instead he stared at his nineties-era desk with the compass-etched epitaph *Baz woz 'ere* and wondered why people bothered carving their names like that.

Were they so unsure of their own relevance that they had to leave a nametag to prove they existed? Oh it was all so stupid! All so pointless. He'd long realised that school was little more than a holding pen for morons and he shouldn't waste energy trying to understand it or them. Only a few more weeks, he told himself, then he'd be rid of it for good.

There were no revision classes that afternoon, so Ocean went home. Though it was Wednesday lunchtime, the time zone at home was set for Saturday night. The curtains were drawn and Match of the Day was on playback. Lager can. Smouldering ashtray. Cigarette gasping out its last grey breaths. And there he was, tarnishing the sofa like a spilt drink. Andy.

'What are you doing home?'

Without taking his eyes from the screen, Andy lifted up an arm in a cast.

'Ouch.' Ocean resisted the urge to smile. 'How did you do that?'

Andy liberated his good hand, reached for his lager, saw it away and belched. 'Rather not talk about it. Fetch us another would you?'

*Fetch it yourself you waste of space.* But no. He'd promised to make more of an effort, so off he went. He didn't mind mainlining alcohol to Andy; perhaps it would even hasten his demise.

'Cheers.' Andy put the can in the nook of his elbow and hissed it open. Ocean felt a perverse sort of pleasure at Andy's discomfort, but then ...

'Andy, how are you going to work with your hand like that?'

'Can't put up scaffolding with a broken paw. Got to wait for it to heal, haven't I?'

'And for money? You'll do what exactly?'

'The boys will keep the business going and your Mum'll tide us over in the meantime.'

He clenched his teeth. 'I'm going for a swim.'

Shoreham Beach was a two mile-long peninsula. With sea views, the houses on the south side commanded million pound price tags but the Daley's own place on the north side was a different story. The house itself was okay; a sixties-built terrace with tired plastic cladding on the front. Instead of sea, their house overlooked the Adur. Across the river was a strip of corrugated warehouses: home improvements, tile and plumbing merchants, and a yard piled with aggregates. If you craned your neck you could also get the pleasures of Shoreham power station's massive smoke stack which was about as welcome on the skyline as a giant middle finger. But all in all, it was a two-minute stroll to the sea and how many places could boast that?

Towel slung over his shoulder, Ocean cut through the residential streets that made up the nucleus of Shoreham Beach. Today the sea was a deep blue, frilled with white breakers. The breeze was too light for the windsurfers but a couple of kite surfers were skipping over the sea. Not too much traffic to contend with then. Pebbles crunched under his feet. He dropped his towel by a patch of lunar cabbage-like vegetation and wildflowers, hid his keys under and kicked off his flip-flops.

Inhale. Salty air. A lungful. Goggles lowered. And go! His feet spiked the shallows, icy water wrapped his calves, his knees, until the weight of water rugby-tackled his legs and in

3

he dived. The cold stung, hurt even, a pinching behind the ears. Murky blue. He flipped onto his back and looked up at the rippling glass of the sea's ceiling. Tendrils tickled at his spine. Sea grass. He let bubbles escape one at a time. As each bubble rose and died, he felt a little better, like a poison leaching out. Andy, his GCSEs and his mollycoddling excuse for a school suddenly weren't so bad. How could anything be bad down here?

He was a strong swimmer and fell into an easy rhythm that took him farther out to sea. After twenty minutes of front-crawl, he reached the yellow buoy that marked out the shipping lane for the nearby harbour. He rapped it twice with his knuckles and pulled his goggles up on his forehead. He loved the deep heady vertigo the water offered. In return he gave himself to all he couldn't control; the current, the tide, the wind, the waves and the marine life that ghosted around him. He was just another piece of matter in an unfathomable mass of sea.

The people on the beach were irrelevant dots. Overhead: a droning sound. He spied it. A Tiger Moth aircraft. Ocean leant back, letting waves lap over him as he watched the plane cut through the sky above. There was a dark shape on top of one of the wings. He righted himself to better see. It was a wing-walker, arms outstretched, whooping with joy over the sound of the propellers. So free, so daring. Ocean wished he were up there, that he was the daredevil wing-walker. The plane swooped down and performed an elegant spin, levelled out and swapped the blue of the sky for the lush green of the South Downs. It was with a pang of sadness, an estrangement, that the plane left his field of vision.

Mum might be home by now. He would have to try and talk to her again about Andy. He slipped down his goggles and set off back to shore.

Ocean had just got out of the shower when he heard the front door. Still dripping wet, he wrapped a towel around his waist and ran down to the kitchen. Mum was unpacking shopping from a Co-op bag.

'Well hello there. Who's this hunk that's come to welcome me home?'

Ocean couldn't hide his disapproval. 'Urgh Mum, weird.'

She grinned. 'Well, I can't help it if my son's handsome.'

He grabbed a cereal box and put it away. 'I wanted to catch you before you go to tennis.'

'Oh, I'm not going tonight.'

'What? You never miss it when the weather's like this. Not that I'm complaining or anything. It'd be good to have you in.'

She loaded cheese and milk into the fridge. 'Uh-huh.'

There was something mechanical in her voice, like her mind was elsewhere. 'Mum, is everything alright?'

She shut the fridge door and sighed. 'Well I suppose you'll hear about it sooner or later anyway.'

Now he was on guard. 'Hear about what?'

'Just a silly misunderstanding is all.'

He folded his arms.

'Andy got it into his head that Harvey from the club was flirting with me.'

Ocean had long lost track of all the tennis people Mum talked about. Each a small jigsaw piece in a changing puzzle he had never quite been able to put together. 'And Harvey is?'

'The new club coach.'

5

'R-ight,' Ocean nodded. 'I get it... so Andy's broken hand—'

'Correct. He's opting not to go to the club for a little while and well, me too. At least until it all dies down.'

'So, he's banned himself from the club? The genius of self-banned Andy. Mum, I know I said I'd stop giving you a hard time over him, but—'

'Oh shush,' she interrupted, 'in a way it's quite romantic when you think about it.'

'Romantic?' his voice rose. The kitchen spotlights caught the whites of her eyes and made her look dopey and wistful. She was hopeless and as much as he tried, Ocean just didn't get it. Andy was so repulsive, so tanned and oily-looking it made you want to wash your hands every time you looked at him. He was a worthless toad, why couldn't she see it too?

'Well. You know what I think.' Ocean stared at the floor. A small pool of water had formed under his feet as if the conversation were melting him. He grabbed a kitchen towel and trod it onto the puddle.

Mum ruffled his hair and planted a kiss on his forehead.

'You're such a sweetie, looking out for me. You'll be a heart-breaker, I just know it.'

'What an aspiration,' he meant it as a joke, but it came out petulant.

'Listen honey. With Andy's hand being out of action for a while we thought, seeing as you're finishing your exams next week that you could...'

He saw where this was going. It wasn't the first time she had suggested he work with Andy's crew during the holidays.

'Oh Mum, no way.'

'Hear me out, would you? It would be a chance for my two favourite boys to spend some time together. You're always outside, you'd like it.'

Ocean couldn't imagine a worse way to spend summer.

'I'll think about it,' he lied.

# 2

# BIOLOGY

Ocean couldn't stand exam time. The exams themselves were fine but the hysteria that surrounded them was insufferable. There was a group of girls in his year group who were particularly annoying, insisting on how little work they'd done when secretly they'd done loads and would act all shocked when a bunch of A stars padded down with the doormat mail in six weeks' time. There were a few wired boys who'd been up cramming since five, making it through on coffee and energy drinks and looked like they might break at any second. The nerds made everyone else panic by wandering around before the exam, testing people on obscure potential questions just to show off how much *they* knew. Then there were the nervous wrecks with their lucky charms for their desks: pencil trolls, cuddly toys and badges. He guessed they would cry afterwards about how bad it was and go home to that god-awful parental conversation about GCSEs not being the be all and end all.

And then there was him. He studied, of course he did, but didn't boast about it, nor claim the hours he studied weren't enough, because at the end of the day, who did he have to blame but himself if it didn't all work out? So far, he felt he'd done pretty well and wasn't about to pretend otherwise. He'd been wrongly accused by some of arrogance, cockiness even. It was just well-placed confidence. That was all. Why should he have to lie to people just for the sake of appearing modest? It was fake.

The final exam was biology, that very afternoon. Ocean spent the morning revisiting the past three years of exam papers and was going over his mind maps when the doorbell went.

He didn't stir. Mum was in, so was self-banned Andy. He rocked back on his chair. A conversation droned below. Who'd stopped by? He went to the window. There was a shiny black car on the street. American maybe. Too low-slung and cool for England. Curious, he crept halfway down the stairs and caught the tail end of a conversation.

'—can't see him. Get out of here,' Mum whispered in harsh tones.

'How will you stop me? Tail him around 24/7?' A man's voice. One he didn't recognise.

'He's got an important exam today and doesn't need any distractions, least of all you! Leave this instant, I'm warning you!'

'He might want to see me, have you ever considered that?'

'This is the last time I'll say it or I'm calling the police. Leave and never come back. I mean it.'

The man laughed. 'Whatever happened to the peace-loving hippy? I'll see you around Skye.'

Ocean tiptoed down a couple more steps, just in time to catch a glimpse of a long black leather coat. Were they in some sort of trouble?

'Mum, who was that?'

Startled, she looked up at him. 'Nobody honey. Go on, get your things and I'll drop you at school.'

'Is everything okay? It sounded—'

'Everything's fine,' she snapped and glanced back at the door. When she turned back her face had softened. 'Come on O, it's your exam. Let's get you there in plenty of time. Go get your things.'

He wouldn't push it. She'd insist he focus on his exams. Later maybe. He grabbed his bag from his room and went to the window. The black car was gone.

The sports hall housed the whole year group. The tables were arranged in a rectangular, symmetrical formation with aisles for the invigilators to prowl. Ocean stowed his phone, took his seat and nodded to Sam who played guard in the basketball team. This year, they'd won the league a second time with Ocean flexing between Forward and Centre, unable to decide which suited him best. Ocean loved winning, but it was much like the other sports he played for the school. It was competitive and a physical challenge, even fun at times, but sport never appealed enough to commit his life to it. After all, they were just games.

Right now the basketball nets were pushed back, though the scoreboard still showed the score from their last game, a whipping of local rivals Worthing High School. Mr Draper cleared his throat and gave the usual pre-exam speech. No phones, no talking, fill in your name and student ID, etcetera, etcetera. Ocean closed his eyes, stilled his wandering mind and got his head in the zone. He pushed out all the things that could distract him; basketball, scaffolding for Andy, the stranger in the black car and visualised his mind maps.

The clock hit the hour and the test began with a cacophony of turning paper. Ocean got to work. He almost laughed. Most of the questions were recycles or variants on past papers. It was about as difficult as a swim round the buoy: easy if you were prepared and knew what you were doing. He finished with half an hour to spare and checked his answers, adding up the total of all the ones he was positive he was right and marking all the ones he was unsure about as wrong. He estimated his score to be about the eighty per cent mark, not bad going at all.

Time was called and the papers collected in. He looked around at the smiling faces. They'd done it, finished. A long summer stretched ahead and he found himself grinning. Sam caught his eye and gave him a questioning thumbs up or thumbs down.

Ocean gave a thumbs-up and pointed back at Sam, you?

So-so, came the reply. *Liar, bet he's aced it.*

The last papers were collected in. Everyone got ready to spring up. Some perhaps wouldn't be back in school ever again. Him too? It was a wild thought, and a thrill ran through him. Could he really stomach another two years of being told to tuck his shirt in and being treated like a child?

'Congratulations ladies and gents, you may now all leave and have a well-earned summer rest.' Mr Draper bellowed. Everyone got up at once and scrambled towards the exit. 'Fitzsimmons! No running!'

Ocean joined the jostling crowd of students and stepped out into the sunshine. Exams were over. A whole summer lay ahead of him. He ran to catch up to Sam and a group of his classmates. They were high-fiving and someone had their phone up, streaming Alice Cooper's *School's out for Summer* but it was so tinny and quiet he started singing the words.

*'No more teachers! No more rule books!'*

Someone else joined in, and soon everyone in the field was yelling:

*'Schooooooooool's out for Sum-mer!'* fists pumping in the air.

Once the song was finished, nobody knew what to do. The lad with the phone put on another track, but it was met with boos and he quickly switched it off. The crowd broke off into smaller groups and Ocean walked with a few of his classmates, letting them talk.

'What do we do now?' someone said.

'Get trashed?'

'Bri-ghton! Get ready to be owned!'

'You coming O?'

Ocean looked at their expectant faces, he could read them all, thinking that he was going to make an excuse, say no. He was half-tempted to say yes just to wrong-foot them but he couldn't pretend he liked spending the night drinking cans of Red Stripe on the beach, plucking up the confidence to try in the pubs where they were a bit lax on ID'ing people.

'Probably not guys, but text me later and let me know where you're at just in case.'

'Sure.'

At least he didn't have to deal with any banter about it. Not to his face at least. Alone, Ocean crossed the school field. He had different thoughts on unwinding after exams. He'd run home, get uncomfortably hot and then dive in the sea for his swim. The tide times app on his phone told him it was hitting mid-tide in half an hour. An easy jog back. He changed quickly behind a hedge, got out his headphones, stretched out his calves and hammys and set off at a gentle pace.

The road that ran parallel to the field was lined with parked cars, mostly belonging to the sixth formers. There were a few couples leaning up against the school fence, holding hands and kissing. The drumbeats of Jack White's *Blunderbuss* came in and each foot thudded away the exam adrenaline. After a hundred metres or so, something made him stop and double take. He walked back to it. It was empty, but parked up right outside his school. The black car.

He paused his music, took his ear buds out. It was definitely the same one. Had to be. He cupped his hands and pressed his face to the glass. The seats were blood-red leather. Instead of a normal gearstick knob there was a small skull, silver and glinting. In the back, crumpled brown bags of McDonald's take-out.

'Quite a beaut isn't she?'

He jumped. The first thing he saw was his own surprised face reflecting in the guy's night-black shades. He was tall, six-three maybe with the added height of a tan fedora hat. From his grey-white beard, Ocean guessed he was in his fifties. The long leather coat and disarming smile made him look pretty formidable.

'Sorry. I was just looking at your car.'

'Course you were, what hot-blooded man wouldn't want to see a '69 Mustang up close and personal?'

Ocean was surprised, the guy had a slight Welsh accent, not what he'd expected at all. He considered sticking his headphones back in and wishing him a good day, but he was just too curious.

'You came to our house today, didn't you?'

13

The man put a cigarette in his mouth and lit it with a chunky golden lighter. 'I did,' he said through the smoke.

'Why?'

'Plenty of reasons.'

Ocean crossed his arms. 'Care to enlighten me?'

'For one, I wanted to see you. Your Mam wasn't too happy about that I can tell you.'

'Yeah, I was watching from the stairs.'

'I know you were.'

Was it not being able to see the guy's eyes or the way he said the words "I know you were" that creeped him out most? Either way, he was out. Time to pull the ripcord on this one, try Mum for answers later.

'Well, you've seen me now,' he put one of his ear buds back in. 'Enjoy your car. You're right, it is a beaut.'

The man took a drag. 'I could give you a lift?'

'Getting into cars with strangers? Please, I've just done eleven exams, I'm not about to get that one wrong.'

'Family aren't strangers, Ocean.'

The headphones fell from his hands. 'What do you mean, family?'

The man held out his hand. 'Ocean, I'm your Uncle Frank.'

# 3

# UNCLE FRANK

They weren't doing thirty and even then the engine had a back-of-the-throat growl to it, like it wanted you to know it was capable of more. The first couple of minutes passed in silence. Ocean's head was so crammed with questions he couldn't seem to prise one out.

'Well you're chatty,' Uncle Frank said, breaking him from his thoughts.

'Just thinking. So ... Uncle Frank ... It feels so weird calling you *Uncle*.'

'Charming. But while we're on the subject of names, I can't believe Jack let your Mam call you Ocean, but then they always were chalk and cheese.'

'At least it's not a boring name like, I dunno, Frank.'

'Touché,' Uncle Frank wound down the window a crack. Seagulls chirruped. Frank leant forward, squinting skywards. 'I swear if those things crap on my car I'll pick them off one by one with a sniper rifle.'

Ocean found himself smiling. 'It's not a question of if, but when.'

Disapproval hummed in Uncle Frank's throat. The Mustang stopped at the traffic lights; prams and cycles crossed the high street and rolled onto the footbridge that straddled the sparkling Adur.

'Why didn't you come to Dad's funeral?' The question left his lips like an arrow. Direct, pointed.

Uncle Frank whistled. 'Now that's the first sensible thing you've asked me.' Their eyes met. 'But I'm not sure I should tell you.'

'Why?'

'I need to know how far I can trust you. What did your Mam say?'

Ocean shrugged. 'She couldn't get hold of you, something like that.'

'True enough.'

'And if I promise to keep it to myself?'

Uncle Frank chewed on his lip. 'I was in prison in Bolivia.'

'You what? What for?'

The lights blinked amber and Uncle Frank pulled away. 'Now that I cannot tell you. Not yet anyway.'

Bolivia, Ocean thought, it must have been drug trafficking.

'It wasn't drugs, if that's what you were thinking,' Uncle Frank said.

'No,' he couldn't hide the defensiveness in his voice. 'So, when did you get out?'

'Three months and change. Thought I'd get the business up and running before I came to see you.'

'Not the same business that got you imprisoned in Bolivia, I hope?' Ocean ventured.

Uncle Frank smiled. 'I've learnt from my mistakes. No, this one is really interesting. Let me ask you something. At your

16

school do you find your classes have to go at an average pace so the slowest lambs can keep up with the flock?'

'Definitely. It's better when we're streamed into sets, but still … I feel like I'm way ahead of most kids, treading water while they catch up.'

'Exactly!' Uncle Frank enthused. 'Imagine an educational model that focuses just on the elite few and stretches them to meet their infinite potential! That's what I've set up. It's a special kind of summer school in the Midlands to prove the concept.'

Ocean was taken aback. 'You're in education?' Uncle Frank looked more like someone who owned a dodgy nightclub.

'I'm rescuing brilliance from the menace of institutionalised mediocrity. Our students behave and are treated like adults. They get the very best equipment and you know what else? There's even a funding programme in place so we actually pay the students.'

'Wh-at? No way.'

'I know right? It's crazy. But here's the thing,' Uncle Frank tapped the steering wheel with his thumb, 'it's entry by recommendation only. What do you think?'

Silence dangled for a few moments before Ocean gathered his meaning, 'What? You mean me?'

'Of course. That's why I'm here.'

'Do I have a HELP ME! sandwich board hanging around my neck or something?'

'Huh?'

'Mum's trying to get me to work as a scaffolder with Andy all summer. I've barely put my pen down and I'm getting the hard sell from somewhere else.'

'Ocean. There's no hard sell. It's an offer on the table for you to pick up or not. Choose greatness, get some money and get away from Shoreham, or don't.'

'But I hardly know you.'

'I did see you a few times when you were a little sprat if that helps? Give it some thought. No pressure.' Uncle Frank reached into his pocket, pulled out a business card and handed it to Ocean. It was black with *Hinckley Farm Summer School* stencilled in neat white lettering. Frank pulled up outside his house and sighed.

'Oh crap. Here comes trouble.'

Before Ocean could ask what he meant, Mum's stricken face appeared on the driver's side. She rapped her knuckles on the window. Uncle Frank wound it down.

'Afternoon Skye, before you get your knickers in a twist I saw your boy walking home and offered him a—'

'Ocean Daley, get out of the car this instant.'

The surname was employed so he did as he was told.

'Shall I leave the engine running or are you going to invite me in for a coffee?'

'Ocean. Here. Now.'

But Ocean stood his ground. He wasn't some damn dog.

'If not coffee, a whiskey would do!' Frank called.

'Bye Uncle Frank.'

'Don't you talk to him!'

The car pulled away. Ocean stuffed the business card into his pocket.

'You've got some explaining to do mister.'

Ocean was incredulous. 'Me? *I've* got explaining to do?'

Mum wagged a finger in his face. He couldn't remember seeing her this cross. 'Too right you do, getting into a car with him!'

He pulled at a tuft of hair at the back of his head. 'Well what do you expect? You've not given me a good reason why I shouldn't see my own uncle. He came to see me this morning and you said it was nobody.'

'He's worse than a nobody! He didn't even come to your father's funeral.'

Ocean opened his mouth to defend Uncle Frank, but remembered his promise not to mention the prison. It would hardly have helped matters anyway. 'Maybe he had his reasons.'

'Don't defend him. What did he want from you?'

'Want? Nothing, he just gave me a lift. Wanted to know how I was.'

'Huh! As if he cares. I don't believe that for one second, what did he want?'

'I told you! Nothing!'

'That man is bad news Ocean. Always was, always will be.'

Andy appeared in the hallway, remote in his good hand. 'What's all the shouting for? I'm trying to watch TV.'

Ocean glared at Mum and shook his head. 'You must be right then, because clearly *you're* such a good judge of character.'

He squeezed between them and ran up the stairs.

'Hey, don't talk like that to your mother!' Andy yelled after him.

'Leave him,' Mum said.

Breath heaving and hot from the argument, Ocean slammed the door and then hated having done so. Why was he acting like some spoilt teenager? In his pocket was the answer. From the business card, he entered Uncle Frank's name and number in his phone and paused over the save button. It wasn't like anyone checked his phone or anything but still ... it didn't hurt to be careful. He deleted Frank's name and thought on an alternative moniker. The only thing that came to mind was that stupid chain of Italian restaurants called Frankie and Benny's. He went with it. Benny.

He cut up the business card, binned the bits and got changed into his swimming trunks. He'd nearly made it to the front door when Mum pulled him back.

'Young man, I think you owe Andy an apology.'

He squeezed his towel as hard as he could, using it as a stress ball.

'You're right. I was rude.'

Best to get it over with quickly, like swallowing medicine or ripping a plaster. He ducked his head in the lounge. The curtains were drawn despite it being a reasonable day outside.

'Andy.'

Andy looked up. 'What?"

'Sorry for what I said back there, I didn't mean it.'

Andy shrugged. 'It's fine. Be as horrible as you like to me, just not to your Mum, okay?'

For a split second he nearly liked the guy. 'Think I can handle that.'

Mum was waiting in the hallway, a smile fixed on her face. 'Good lad.'

He nodded. 'Right, I'm off for a swim.'

'Wait, you didn't even tell me how your exam went?'

'Oh yeah, fine. Good actually.'

She sighed and fiddled with his fringe. 'Your dad would've been so proud of you. Have you thought any more about which A-Levels you want to do?'

'Please can you give the A-Levels a rest? I've told you I still haven't decided for sure that I'll go back. I'll think about it, just stop pushing.'

'Alright crabby,' she made her hands into pincers and grabbed at him, a joke she'd played plenty of times over the years.

'Hey,' he laughed, 'stop that! Mum, I really should go, it's heading mid to high so ...'

'Alright, just one last thing,' she lowered her pincers, 'tomorrow, it would mean a lot to me if you gave it a go with Andy. Go to the site with him and work for the day,' she leant in and whispered behind her hand, 'might get him off the couch and feel a bit better about himself.'

Ocean stared blankly. His lips started moving. 'Okay.' And before he could retract it, she planted a kiss on his forehead.

'Such a sweet boy.'

The second he was out the door, he looked around for a lamppost to head-butt. Why oh why had he agreed to spend the day with Andy? By the time he got to the beach, he was ready to use the water as a punch bag. He dove in like a torpedo and beat the water with his fists as he swam.

# 4

# POLES APART

The next morning Ocean woke hoping for an out with the scaffolders. Shoreham often served up rain and high winds but when he drew back the curtains there was only glorious wall-to-wall sunshine. Was even the weather against him?

Andy was waiting downstairs. The look? Classic Andy: Jeans, Timberland boots and string vest accessorised with a flask and a copy of *The Sun.*

'Nice uniform,' Ocean said, 'I don't have to read that do I? Just so you know, I'm cool with not fitting in.'

'No, this is for me smartass. What do you think I'll be doing while you're working?'

'I dunno, maybe telling me what I actually need to do, make sure I put my harness on right, that sort of thing.'

Andy scoffed. 'Harness? Ha!'

Was he joking? But Ocean suddenly couldn't recall if he'd ever seen scaffolders wearing harnesses before. Heights didn't phase him but he'd sooner try wing-walking. An experienced pilot he could trust, but Andy's cowboys?

In the van, Ocean clipped in and fiddled with the radio. Andy put the key in the ignition and stared through the windscreen for a few seconds.

'Bollocks.'

'What?'

Andy lifted up his cast. 'I don't think I can drive.'

Ocean sighed. 'I hope that Harvey bloke was worth it.'

'Not really,' Andy massaged his cast, 'turns out he couldn't have had the hots for your mum.'

'Why not?'

'Apparently he's gay.'

Ocean couldn't stop himself laughing. 'You idiot.'

'Alright, alright. So I'm an idiot.' Andy shook his head and grinned sheepishly. 'Can you drive us to site 0?'

'I'm sixteen.'

'That's too young is it? I forget the legal age.'

He was tempted, it was only four months until he was seventeen and the early practice might do him good.

'I've never tried, but I could give it a go, is it far?'

'Goring. About eight miles too far if you can't drive.'

A taxi dropped them off at a block of flats a half-hour later. Andy paid the fare.

'It's alright, we'll get one of the lads to drop us home later and I'll just take that taxi off your wages.'

Ocean couldn't believe the cheek and opened his mouth to protest until he noticed Andy's face. 'Waaah, I was just joshing—you should have seen the look on your Chevy Chase.' He clapped Ocean on the back.

Ocean forced a smile. 'Yeah good one.' It was going to be a long day.

The flats were only a couple of blocks back from the seafront and suffered from the same winter battering as the buildings on Shoreham Beach. The sea salt and winds were unforgiving, no matter how well built the structures were;

walls crumbled, paintwork flaked, balconies cracked and railings rusted. Scaffolding was an industry in constant demand up and down the coast, making Andy's business partnership a fairly reliable one. Ocean didn't know if its success was luck or design on Andy's part. He'd like to think it was luck but swarthy and unlikable as Andy was, Ocean had to admit that he did possess a measure of low cunning.

The Lightning Fast Scaffolding Crew Ltd. truck was parked in the forecourt of the flats. The words *Your erection is in reliable hands*, were written under the emblem of a lightning bolt. What moron thought of that? Ocean wondered.

'I thought of that,' Andy said without a trace of shame, pointing at the slogan.

'Andy, it's things like that make it much harder for me to like you.'

Behind the driver's cab, scaffold poles were stacked high. Three of the Lightning Crew were already there, topless and sweating. They all had tattoos, random shapes and colours over their torsos, an urban rash that took each of its victims in a slightly different fashion.

Ocean was introduced as "Sean" to Baz, Stewart and Dean. He wondered if it was the same wistful *Baz woz 'ere* who had once etched his name in the lecture theatre desks at Shoreham Academy. The thought made him shiver all over as if he were watching a possible life choice unfold.

Baz woz 'ere set up a portable amp and turned on some pounding dance music, nodding in time as he dialled it up beyond house party level.

'Andy, is that alright?'

'What?' Andy cupped his ear in jest.

Ocean pointed at the speaker. 'Is that alright? It's not even nine yet.'

Andy gave the thumbs up. 'Yeah, the lads need a bit of music. Makes them work faster.'

Above, at one window an old lady with curlers in her hair was shaking her head at them. At another, a woman rocked a crying baby in her arms. Ocean's face reddened with embarrassment, his only escape was to distract himself with work.

There were no hard hats, no high-vis jackets and definitely no harnesses. His safety gear consisted of a pair of gloves. The poles were all numbered with bright pink spray-paint. It was his task to help unload and pass them up when instructed. He was surprised and even impressed by how hard they worked, never ambling, always walking fast with quick-hand offs as if they were being competitively timed. It was physical work and he liked that aspect of it. But the awful dance music, the lad jokes and the wolf whistles whenever a woman strolled down the street were embarrassing beyond belief.

At lunch, Baz woz 'ere, Dean and Stewart went for a walk to a sandwich shop. Ocean hadn't brought any money or lunch with him, so he sat with Andy, gratefully accepting half of his cheese and ham sandwich.

'Sometimes you can be alright.'

'Thanks,' Andy said, leaning back and letting the sun glisten off his berry-brown face. He pulled a cigarette from behind his ear and lit it. They sat in silence for a moment.

'You enjoying the work?'

'There are things about it which are alright I guess. Being outside, doing physical work.'

'I sense a big hairy but coming.'

'However,' Ocean sidestepped the trap, 'could I do this all summer?' he shook his head. 'I'm sorry. I know it's your business and everything, but it just isn't for me.'

Andy tapped ash from the end of the cigarette into a Coke can. 'I know it's not. Listen, I'm glad you gave it a go. Really, it's one more day for my hand to heal.'

'What do we tell Mum?'

'I'll tell her you were next to useless if you like, that I wouldn't take you on if she paid me.'

He couldn't believe how cool Andy was being. 'Thanks Andy, really, I mean it.'

'No problemo.' Andy posted the cigarette end into the can and then threw it into a nearby flowerbed. 'So if not this, what will you do all summer?'

Ocean didn't say anything, but he had an idea.

# 5

# INFLUENCE

O cean's kneecaps protruded out of the bathwater like two smooth river deltas. The warm water teased out the pleasing ache in his shoulders and arms—the levy for a day's graft with the Lightning Crew. In all, he concluded, the day had gone well. Most surprising of all, his opinion of Andy had gone up a notch. From zero, Andy was now on one.

Ocean was no fool. Mum and Andy had been together for eighteen months already and unless she came to her senses soon, he'd end up with self-banned Andy for a stepdad. The very idea made him squirm, like spider-webs catching on your face. God he hoped he'd be out of here by then, in his own place with a life of his own. Ocean held his breath, let his head sink under and let the bubbles escape one by one.

Jack Daley had been a strong and wiry man. As a father, he tried to play the disciplinarian but he wasn't around enough to make it stick. His jokes were painfully funny and too rude to be aired in front of Mum. At night he allowed himself a double whisky; his favourite being a single malt whose nostril burning fumes would make Ocean's head spin but his father could gulp down like iced water on a scorching day. He was an arms-length man, even with Mum. Growing up, Ocean sensed a respect between his parents, but never love. Never passion. With his father being home some six weeks a year there was almost no point in keeping up the pretence of a family unit the rest of the time. It was fun to play-act for those brief weeks he was home. To have barbecues, throw the frisbee on the beach and watch movies together.

Dad's absence had another effect too. His form tutors said Ocean had a "natural aptitude" for learning. In fact, it was a by-product of the compressed time windows in which Ocean had to show off all he'd learnt to his dad. Yes, he had been one of those yelping, 'hey Dad, look, look at me, look, did you see?' kids for a while, nauseating though it was to admit now.

At first it was just some dumb trick with the football but Dad seemed so genuinely impressed that the next time he was home, Ocean showed him how he could hold his breath for two minutes underwater; then, some website he'd designed for *Rocky* aficionados with their favourite quotes and stills; shooting free throws blind-folded; swimming with him to the buoy for the first time and a hundred other things over the years. So Ocean wasn't convinced about it being a *natural* aptitude. It implied a genetic advantage from birth and Mum's solid tennis game and bangle wearing dabbles at yoga weren't exactly compelling evidence for that. But from the great Mr Jack Daley himself? Maybe, Ocean didn't rightly know.

Dad never really spoke about his job, so Ocean had no idea if he was on the ground operations or something tactical in the background. Nature/nurture arguments only made him yawn anyway, wasn't it always a mix of both? Regardless, Ocean's knack of challenging himself to master new skills had

28

become a habit that could not be broken, even when they received the news that would change their lives forever.

It happened four years ago. There was a knock at the door. A crew cut stood in military uniform, cap tucked under his arm and stamped his feet on the mat. Ocean was thirteen and had seen enough films to know what it meant. Mum dropped to her knees and bawled her eyes out right there in the hallway. He remembered resting a hand on her shoulder, giving it a squeeze and helping to pull her up.

What did he feel? Numb, mostly. Confused. A vague, ungraspable sadness. He felt he should be reacting differently, beating his fists on the wall, sending hate mail to the Prime Minister, but he couldn't fake something he didn't feel. Then he realised that this must be shock, his reaction and feelings were simply jammed up, delayed. On the Internet it said that this was a common reaction to have. He stayed strong for Mum, helped with the funeral arrangements, did the little he could and waited for it to hit, waited for the approaching bells and rumble of the freight train in the night, waited to be mown down by it all ... because that was what was supposed to happen. Wasn't it? Only it didn't come, not for him. Maybe it was because Afghanistan was so far away or that his father had been gone for so long that he felt detached. All the same, this emotional void was black, cold and unexplored and he dared not look too deeply. He was afraid of what he might find.

Since his father's death, there was only one moment in which he'd felt exposed: those few minutes spent in the car with Uncle Frank. It was like looking down from a great height and feeling a giddy rush of vertigo. He couldn't explain it, but the instinct to run away from it wasn't there, in fact it was just

29

the opposite. Uncle Frank was different from anyone he'd ever met and not necessarily in a good way. The fact Ocean wasn't sure about Frank just made him all the more intriguing. As odd as a Summer School sounded, he could get away from home and get everyone off his back in one fell swoop.

When Mum arrived home from work, Ocean got the plates out the oven, lit the candles on the kitchen table. Mum's masseuse bag hit the carpet with a slap.

'Hi Boys! Something smells good.'

'It's me,' Andy yelled from the lounge.

Ocean drained the jasmine rice and filled a small bowl with it. With quick hands, he tipped the bowl upside down on the plate, gave it a tap like a sandcastle bucket and lifted it away. A circular mound of rice rested, steaming on the plate. Perfection.

'Come sit down,' he shouted and ladled the Thai green curry onto the first plate.

'Oh my word! This looks amazing,' Mum said, unhoofing her shoes. 'Andy, I hope you're wearing your elasticated trousers!'

Andy padded in, cigarette drooping between his lips. '*Eastenders* is on in a mo, can't we ...' he took it out and stubbed it on a saucer. 'Oh, wow, this looks great mate.'

As a final touch Ocean squeezed a bit of lime over the rice and a leaf of coriander to decorate.

'Sit,' Ocean commanded, 'let's eat.'

'What a treat, what's in it?' Mum asked.

'Broccoli, aubergines, baby sweetcorn, cashews a few other things.'

'What, no meat?' Andy hissed open a bottle of beer and slid onto his chair.

'You know Andy, It wouldn't hurt you to go veggie a couple of days a week. I read this article about how the pollution caused by the meat industry is a major contributor to glob—'

'Not this again. Global warming's probably bollocks and if it isn't then I'd welcome a bit of warmer weather in Blighty.'

Ocean shovelled some food into his mouth to stop himself from telling Andy what an ignorant hammerhead he was. He Zen chewed, recognising that they'd had variations on this debate dozens of times already—another one wasn't likely to change Andy's mind. Plus, there were bigger things at play.

'Fair enough Andy. Just hope you like the dinner, that's all, meat or none.'

'Well I think it's lovely,' Mum said soothingly and tucked into the food with a series of *mmms*.

As they ate, Andy gave a generous account of their day together and Ocean was doubly glad he hadn't chosen to pick a fight. Andy reported that Ocean had worked hard, that he'd been really proud of him but the Lightning Crew had a quiet patch over the next few weeks and paying for an extra pair of hands didn't really make financial sense. After all, the UK was still flirting with recession, he added.

'So, if you won't be working with Andy, what will you do O?'

Ocean pronged a stem of broccoli and stared at it like it might have the answer. 'Well, I do have an offer I wanted to talk to you about actually.'

'Oh?' Mum put her fork down on the plate, chewed and met his eye, like she'd been expecting this the whole time.

'Yeah,' he pushed a mound of rice into the sauce and got ready to roll out his story. There wasn't any information about Hinckley Farm Summer School online, probably because it was too new, so he had decided a simpler fiction would be easier to digest. 'It's an activity centre. You know, the kind of place that does paintballing, archery and that kind of stuff. They need staff for the safety briefings and to clean the equipment, wash coveralls and so on.'

'Sounds ace.' Andy said.

Mum shot Andy a warning stare. 'And who's running this centre?'

This was the part Ocean had been dreading, but he was ready. 'This guy called Benny. He's the dad of one of the boys in the rugby team. A few of them did it last year apparently and learnt loads of skills. It's great work experience for the CV.'

Mum's face softened, she picked up the fork again. 'Sounds interesting.'

'What they offering?' Andy asked.

'Eighty quid a week,' he paused, it was time to throw the spanner in. 'Plus food and board.'

Mum's fork dropped again with a clunk. 'Whoa there! Food and board? Where is this place? I thought you said it was your friend's father?'

'It is, but they're divorced. It's near Leicester.'

Mum looked wide-eyed at Andy. 'That's a long way away from home for a sixteen-year-old.'

Andy shrugged. 'Those South Beach ponces send their kids to boarding school when they're just little sprogs. And Lancing College on the hill, how old are that lot? They're on their own and lots younger than O.'

'It's not the same though Andy, those are schools with structures, staff and procedures.'

'So has the centre Mum. I know it sounds like a big deal, but it really isn't. In a few months I'll be seventeen. I mean, some of the lads who just finished their exams are flying out to Ibiza on their own. What do you think *they're* going to be doing Mum? Charity work? All *I'm* asking is to do a bit of work over the summer, spend more time outdoors, save up a bit.'

She waved her fork at the food. 'Ocean, this is lovely, all of this. Thank you, but I'm really not sure about letting you go.'

It was time to play his trump card. 'I feel like I need a change of scene Mum. I do love it here, but sometimes it all feels so ... close,' he leant forward. 'And if I could do this, I'd definitely feel happier about staying here to do my A-Levels.'

'Oh, he's good,' Andy said, nodding.

But Ocean didn't take his eyes off Mum. She shook her head, lips pursed, covering a smile. It was tipping in his favour. *Say yes.*

'I'll ring every day and if I don't like it or it's not safe I promise I'll be on the first train home.'

'Could be the making of him,' Andy said, quietly enough that it could almost be a thought in her own head.

Mum sighed. 'I must be turning into a soft touch. You better ring me every day like you promise Ocean Daley or I'll drive up there and fetch you back myself.'

He threw his arms around her. Andy winked at him.

As soon as he was able, he bounded up the stairs to his room and called Benny.

# 6

# HINCKLEY FARM

Ocean's canvas bag was packed and ready on the bed. He stared at the text message.

There's a restaurant nearby you know I like.

Meet me there in an hour.

When he'd spoken to Uncle Frank last night, Frank said he would text *exactly* where to meet. Not this! What was he playing at? Ocean had committed Mum's schedule to memory and within the next hour she would be travelling from Hove to Worthing, possibly going through Shoreham town centre. He was annoyed; he did *not* want to be seen getting into the Mustang by her or by anyone who knew them. It was not the time for games. He began typing a reply, telling Uncle Frank to give it up and tell him where to meet, but a thought struck him ... was this a test? He couldn't figure out what purpose it would serve, but then Uncle Frank was different, and that was what he liked about him.

Which restaurant did Frank like? He couldn't recall anything from their conversation in the car or from their brief phone call the night before. The clock on his phone read 2.04pm, giving him fifty-six minutes to work it out and get there. He read the text message again, from Benny. Benny.

Could that be it? Frankie and Benny's? He was positive he hadn't mentioned the alias, but it was possible. He googled the nearest one—it was over in Brighton Marina, too far away.

'A restaurant *I like.*'

What *did* Uncle Frank like? He had weird clothes, a fedora, his Mustang ... his Mustang! Ocean had it! He palmed himself in the forehead for not thinking of it before. Of course it wasn't Frankie and Benny's. It was McDonald's. Perhaps it was a bit of a stretch calling it a restaurant but the take-out rubbish in the back of the Mustang was a clear clue.

Pleased to have worked it out, Ocean gave his room one last look. It was tidy and neat, the bed made. Above the headboard was a black and white poster of Rocky Balboa punching his fist in the air with a quote. It was ... no, it had been, his father's favourite film. They'd watched the *Rocky* movies together each time his dad had leave. Ocean liked the quote, cheesy though it was. *"You are where you are because of the decisions you've made. The choice has always been yours to make. Either choose to be great or choose to be waste."*

'Well Dad,' he said to the poster, 'I'm going to see your brother and I'm choosing to be great.'

He left a hastily scribbled note for Mum, promising to call her later, yanked on his boots, denim jacket and pulled a Brighton & Hove Albion Seagulls cap down low over his eyes. It was a windy day and he walked fast over the footbridge. Rigging ropes pulled and tinkled against the boats moored on the river. The skate park was en route and it was guaranteed to be teeming with kids from school, so he took a small detour one road up and doubled back to McDonald's.

He heard the Mustang before he saw it, easing out the drive-thru. Uncle Frank wound the window down and held up a brown bag in his fist.

'I got you a couple of cheeseburgers.'

Ocean made sure nobody was watching, threw his bag in the back and got in the passenger side. The car smelt salty and warm.

'Thanks.' McDonald's wasn't his favourite, but he'd been too excited to eat lunch and was hungry enough to wolf down both burgers.

It was a long drive to Leicestershire, time in which Ocean's hopes to learn more about Uncle Frank were shot down before they'd even reached the motorway.

'Rules are these. If I decide to share something with you, I'll share it. Badgering me and asking me tons of questions will only serve to piss me off and you do not want to see me pissed off, believe me.'

Frustrating though it was, Ocean paid heed to these rules. There was time enough to get to know Uncle Frank better. They talked mostly about school and Ocean's sports, interrupted by Uncle Frank asking for the *Johnny Cash* CD to be changed for *The Doors*. It was still fairly light when the Mustang took the grit road turning for Hinckley Farm.

'Four hundred acres.'

Four hundred acres? Ocean wondered who owned the land and how Uncle Frank came to be running it so soon after a jail stint ... but guessed that this question would be off limits. Uncle Frank pulled into an open barn where two mud spattered Land Rovers were parked by a small fleet of quad bikes. Ocean couldn't wait to get out and stretch his legs but Uncle Frank gently held him back.

36

'Wait a sec. Listen. You're my nephew but that doesn't mean I can treat you any different from the others. You get that don't you?'

Ocean wanted no free passes. There was a lad at the Shoreham Academy whose Mum taught Geography and was ribbed mercilessly for it. 'Fine by me.'

Ocean got out of the car and did a back bend and enjoyed the agreeable crack. Finally he was away from home and independent. There was a long brick farmhouse veined with ivy and another outbuilding opposite the barn. He heard voices, the sound of laughter.

'You're the last student to get here.'

Ocean rolled his head to the left and to the right, stretching his neck muscles. 'How many of us are there then?'

Uncle Frank scratched his beard. 'Six.'

'Six? Like the number six? The one that comes after five?'

'Yep, half a dozen, including you.'

'Is that all?'

'Hey, that's not bad. We've only been open a couple of months. We can scale the school in the future should we want to.'

'Not sure it counts as a school. More a loungeful.'

'I suppose if you count the three tutors, a cook and me then yes, we're a small but perfectly formed organisation.'

Two students per tutor? He knew that a low ratio of students to tutors was a good recipe for learning; maybe he should have been honest to Mum about what he was doing here. What mother could possibly object to such an education?

'Hey Frank!' A man emerged from the farmhouse. 'I thought I heard that beast of yours purring in the driveway,' his American accent was full of the Deep South.

37

Uncle Frank clinked open his lighter and lit a cigarette. 'Warren, this young man here is Ocean.'

Warren offered his hand. He was dark-skinned with thick jam-jar glasses. He was hard to pin an age to, in his forties or fifties maybe?

'I've heard a lot about you.'

'Have you?' Ocean was surprised Uncle Frank knew enough about him to talk.

'I'm what you Brits call an I.T tutor, but I specialise in advanced coding.'

When Warren smiled it was all pearly white teeth and pink gums. 'That bag all you got?'

Ocean nodded and followed, wondering how good he'd be compared to the other students at coding. He knew some of the basic coding languages from school but didn't know how to do much more than build a basic webpage.

The hallway had a homely smell of smoke and wood. Ocean kicked off his shoes and squeezed his feet into the rich red carpet.

'Nice place.'

Someone was walking down the stairs and Warren inclined his head to see who it was. 'Ah, perfect. Ocean here is another one of our tutors—Scarlet.'

First name terms. How much more grown up than the subservient 'Sir' and 'Miss' he had to employ at school. Scarlet stopped on the bottom step and took him in. She had a roundish face, wrinkled skin and deep set black eyes like those of a doll. Only a few strands of grey hair gave any indication as to her age.

She placed a hand to her mouth. 'My word.'

Ocean felt a shiver run down his spine. 'What?'

'You look so ...' she shook her head.

'Like Frank when he was younger? Warren chipped in. 'Maybe a little.'

Her strawberry-blonde hair bobbed up and down. 'Just so.'

Not the greatest compliment Ocean had ever had, but then he hadn't exactly had a close examination of Frank, he always wore his aviator sunglasses and fedora.

'I'll show you where you're sleeping.'

The room was a dorm with spring bunk beds. He didn't know why, but he'd been expecting his own room and felt foolish, entitled even for having thought it. It was big, the beds spaced far enough apart and plenty of floor space, even accounting for the socks, clothes, toothpaste tubes and deodorant cans strewn across the floor.

'Kaya's the messiest, the boys are actually fairly tidy.'

'That's cool, my room's about the same back home,' he lied. He was pretty OCD when it came to cleanliness and it wouldn't do him any harm to loosen up a bit.

'You're a Seagulls fan?' she motioned to Ocean's baseball cap. 'Pity.'

He smiled and took the cap off and rubbed his hair up. 'You're a Palace fan then?'

'Since I was a little girl,' she sighed, 'my cross to bear. Bathroom's in here,' Scarlet tugged the light, 'not your own personal en suite or anything but if it's busy there's another one down the corridor.'

'Where do the tutors stay?'

'We're in the other building, opposite the barn.'

'And what do you instruct Scarlet?'

She inclined her head. 'My background is in psychology but here I'll be teaching a range of related things.'

Ocean smiled. 'Related to psychology? By definition that could be anything.'

Scarlet raised an eyebrow. 'Frank said you were a clever one. Come on. Let's meet the others; we're all here except Uri, our other tutor. He runs all the physical, outdoorsy things. He's gone to Leicester for supplies and probably gone for a curry,' she spoke behind the flat of her hand conspiratorially, 'he's obsessed with the curry here.'

Three tutors: Warren on I.T, Scarlet on psychology and Uri for sports. Ocean dumped his bag on a free bed and wondered who his bunkmate was. Not a snorer with any luck, though it hardly mattered in a shared room. All it took was one.

After checking in with Mum, he found the group on the back patio. Strangers chattered around a table covered with a bowl of salad, burger buns and sauce bottles. Meat sizzled on a barbecue. Nervous, Ocean took a few steps towards them and the chatter stopped. The students all looked to be about his age and eyed him with undisguised curiosity. Uncle Frank stood up.

'Here he is! Take a seat Ocean. Normally we have a cook, but it's her night off, so we got ourselves a team barbecue—I'm sure you'll approve.'

There was only meat on the barbecue. No peppers. No fish. His heart sank but he wouldn't make a fuss, his quest to eat less meat could wait for a night.

'We'll eat in a second, but first let me introduce you to the rest of the band.' Uncle Frank clapped his hands together. 'You've already met Scarlet and Warren. So let me see if I've got all the names straight myself. We'll start....' he gestured to a brick barbecue where a beefy crew cut was flipping over a row of steaks.

'Here! On drums, all the way from Tulsa, Oklahoma, Drew Anderson!' Everyone around the table clapped, but Drew rolled his eyes.

'Drums? I'm at least worth lead guitar.'

Uncle Frank shook his head. 'See, he's not even been here a week and he already thinks he runs the place!'

Drew pointed a spatula at Uncle Frank. 'You want these babies done rare you better play nice.'

Uncle Frank waved him away. 'Next, on keys, from Johor Bahru in Malaysia, we have Kaya. Stand up sweetie.'

*Ah, the messy one.* He gave Kaya a nod and a smile as everyone else clapped. She had her black hair pinned up and even in the fading light he could see there were plenty of metal piercings on her nose and ears and a tattoo of a scorpion on her neck. She gave him a curt nod and turned her head. Shy or angry?

Uncle Frank smiled. 'Next. From Cádiz, on bass guitar, Dante.'

Ocean held up a hand. 'Hey man.'

Dante had a slightly podgy face and gave Ocean a geeky thumbs up. 'Good to meet you *tío.*'

Next to Dante was a jaundiced looking skinhead, wiry and bony. He wondered where in Uncle Frank's imaginary band this guy would play.

'This one here,' Uncle Frank said, 'is Vasile, from Bucharest,' he screwed his face up in thought, 'yeah, we best put him in charge of the tambourine.'

This drew a laugh from the others and another round of claps. Vasile shot Uncle Frank an evil stare. 'Whatever.'

Before Uncle Frank could speak, the last student stood up and walked over to Ocean and offered him his hand. He was squat, stocky with dark skin and a thin moustache over his lip.

'I'm Claude. From Marseilles. It is a pleasure to meet you.'

He took Claude's hand. 'Likewise.'

'Well someone's got some manners! For that Claude, you get lead guitar.'

Ocean took a spare seat and within moments Drew had deposited a steak on his plate, and one on Uncle Frank's. 'Who gets vocals then Frank?'

Uncle Frank cut into his steak and held the square of meat up. Blood and juice dripped off it. 'Well that'll have to be Ocean now won't it?'

*So much for not showing me any favouritism.* Ocean stared at his steak, coleslaw and salad. 'Oh man, this looks so good,' he said, keen to move on from Frank's imaginary band.

Uncle Frank leant back on his chair, the barbeque flames reflecting back in his shades. 'So what do you think of our little group here?'

Everyone went quiet. Fat sizzled onto the coals. *Why put me at the centre of attention again?*

'It seems great. Definitely a lot more international than I expected,' he answered truthfully, 'who knew Leicestershire was such a draw?'

This brought laughter from around the table. He wasn't sure it was that funny but took the acclaim nonetheless.

They tucked into dinner and Ocean was glad to fade back from the spotlight and listen to the conversation pass around the group. Although the others hadn't long arrived at the school, they talked with the swagger of incumbents. There were jokes about Drew snoring like a bison and some card game they'd played the day before. It didn't bother him; he'd soon be part of it too.

Ocean was helping to stack the plates and cutlery when Drew cleared his throat.

'So Frank,' Drew glanced at Ocean, 'I was thinking, seeing as we're all here now we could play a game? Last One Standing maybe?'

Ocean looked around the table for some clue as to what this was, failing to hide the concern on his face. Last One Standing did not sound like a good thing at all.

Uncle Frank nodded slowly. 'Why not? Warren, seeing as Uri's not here would you mind running it?' he got to his feet and wiped his mouth with a napkin. 'Have fun. Classes start tomorrow.'

'Awesome!' Drew punched his palm in delight. 'Kaya, you get the goggles. And me,' he stared directly at Ocean. 'I'll go get the guns.'

# 7

# LAST ONE STANDING

Two minutes. That was what they were allowed. Ocean tripped on a log but managed to keep his feet. He'd never worn night vision goggles before. This new green world was weird and it was hard to resist the urge to rip his mask off and use the naked eye.

Through a gap in the trees was the central clearing. A helicopter shell lay in the middle, eerie as an alien egg in the green light. Ocean caught movement; a thin beam of light. Kaya was running to her start point in Zone B. He pulled in the muzzle of his own gun and switched off his laser sighting and headed deeper into the wood. At last he found it. The rusted barrel with an 'A' spray-painted on. His knees quivered. He gripped the gun tighter. Somewhere out in the woodland, an owl hooted. Then the shrill starting whistle cut the night.

He crouched and let his eyes adjust a moment more. He was the newest here, an appealing target. Instinct told him to move. The dried mud and rock wasn't the quietest underfoot but it hardly mattered; all he could hear was his own breath echoing around the facemask like *Darth Vader.* When he stopped and held his breath, he earned a few seconds of clean sound. There was the rustle of an animal, a hedgehog perhaps.

After fifty metres of slow, creeping progress he reckoned he was probably in Zone B and slid behind the trunk of a tree.

The rules were pretty simple. He could travel into any of the six zones of the game area. There were no teammates, only targets and two ways to eliminate someone. Firstly, the guns expelled glow-in-the-dark paint pellets at high velocity; a direct hit on your mark and they were out of the game. A second option—and one Ocean thought to be nigh on impossible—was to be so close to your target you could snatch a small flag from the back of your opponent's coveralls. The ultimate goal of course was to be the Last One Standing. Ocean would just settle for not coming last. He felt at his back to check the flag was still there. Ultimate paranoia, of course it was.

The whistle sounded. Yes! Somebody had been eliminated; he wasn't going to finish last! At least that was something. Another part of him admonished himself for being such a coward. *Yeah, well done genius, you managed to hide in the woods for ten minutes.*

At least now there was nothing to lose. The chopper in the middle of the arena felt like the likely spot to find others. Maybe he'd get lucky with a shot or two. Crouched low, he crept from one tree to another, counted out fifteen seconds and moved towards the next trunk. He peered around and snapped straight back into cover.

Someone was there.

The glimpse wasn't enough to tell who it was. Not Drew; the figure was too slight and frighteningly quiet. Kaya or Vasile at a guess. Ocean pressed his gun against his chest, his heart thumping against the metal. Had he been seen? He could round the tree and just start shooting, but that was a risky play. If the target already had a gun pointing in his direction he'd be cooked for sure.

Ninja silent, he crouched and gathered a stone. With an underarm throw he chucked it deep into the undergrowth. It landed with a crash. The moment it did, he rounded the tree and the target was there, back to him, gun pointed at the noise. Perfect. He switched on the laser sighting. The dot and laser-light cut an odd white in his goggles and he traced a line from the floor to the back of his opponent. *Target locked* came a stupid voice in his head from some dumb action movie. *Shuk-Shuk-Shuk.*

Paint exploded all over the target's coveralls like a psychedelic Pollock.

'Ow! Damn it!'

The voice gave it away. Kaya. Ocean hid back behind the tree, flipped off the laser sighting and resisted the urge to yell out a 'Yes!' She'd come across as standoffish at the barbecue and being taken out the game by the newbie was unlikely to improve her mood. She stomped off in search of Warren and within a couple of minutes, the whistle sounded. Four left, including him.

The steady approach was working well thus far, so he stuck with it, progressing through the muddle of trees towards the heart of the game arena. Despite the cool night, his hands were clammy with sweat, finger stiff from holding it trigger-ready. When he arrived at the clearing, he tucked himself behind a pine tree and peeked between the branches at the chopper. No sign of life. The air was rich with earth and pine as he crawled through the bed of fallen needles. He poked the barrel of his gun out and waited. And waited.

Tingly arms. Being stuck in the same position for so long was sending his body to sleep. He wiggled his toes to keep the blood circulating. It occurred to him that if his three opponents were all doing the same as him they'd be out there all night. He risked lighting up his watch for a second. Quarter past midnight! Had they really been playing that long?

More time passed. He went to rub his eyes but his fingers bumped into the goggles. His bladder was uncomfortably full. Five minutes later, he saw something, some black movement on the other side of the clearing. It was the quickest of glimpses, like when you catch a shooting star out of the corner of your eye. It had to be one of the targets. Time to force some action.

Silent as a shadow, he slipped back, grateful for a reason to move his limbs again. He kept to the clearing's fringe until he closed in on the spot. Was he being watched too? He scampered under a man-made barricade of branches and prepared to defend.

Footsteps. He peered over the barricade. A shadow darted between the trees. Clever. Trying drawing him out. He'd have to be careful. He belly crawled around the defence and trained his gun on the spot. As he shuffled a little nearer to the trunk, a twig snapped under the weight of his knee. The shadow bolted.

Crap! Ocean sprang up, following the movement with his gun but he couldn't get a clean shot through the trees. The target didn't dash deeper into the woods as he would have done, but sprinted for the clearing. A trap?

Ocean scurried up, desperately looking for an open shot and with a sinking heart, saw the antlers and the flying hooves of his quarry. A deer.

Struck dumb, he lowered his gun.

'Idiot.'

*Shuk-shuk.*

The dive was instinctive, he waited for the bite of pain but it didn't come. He hit the ground, commando rolled and stayed low. The tree where he'd been standing a split-second before was now covered in paint. He looked up. Drew was firing from the chopper's beaten out window and just as another *shuk-shuk* filled the air, Ocean leapt for cover.

Then all he could hear was a barrage of shots as Drew rained paint pellets at him, but none made it through.

'Damn it!' Drew yelled.

Ocean couldn't believe he'd managed to stay in the game and risked a look. Drew was walking out the helicopter, gun held aloft in submission! What? Had someone else got him?

With his position compromised, there was no time to waste. Ocean crept deep into the woods and then doubled back on himself. The whistle for Drew sounded just as Ocean approached the clearing again. The chopper was just about visible through the trees. Now that was interesting. The paint was mostly on the floor of the machine. The shots must have been angled down. He looked up into the trees. There were plenty of handholds and climbable branches. In fact, the more he thought about it, the more it made sense. He should have thought of it himself.

Ocean ghosted around the trees, looking up this time. The leafy branches overlapped, presenting a thick canopy of such randomness that he couldn't tell what was a natural formation, a human figure, a bird's nest or simply shadow. Not for the first time, he resisted the urge to flip up his facemask and look for himself. He stood in the spot where he guessed the trajectory of the fire had come from to hit the helicopter's floor. Then he saw it. A foot, dangling down.

He locked onto it, moved closer just as the foot silhouette disappeared into darkness again. It was a slip. His pulse raced. The branches spouting from the trunk were especially thick, making it impossible to see if anyone was hiding there. Had he not seen the foot, he never would have known. Ocean took his time—he had no real target to aim at, more an area where he guessed the body to be, so elected not to use the laser sight. Not an easy shot by any means but he had the advantage of surprise. It was time to really open up, cover the area to guarantee a hit.

He closed his left eye, squinted through the sight and squeezed the trigger. *Shuk-Shuk-Shuk*. The pellets exploded with milky splats on the branch. Ocean peppered a volley of shots a little higher.

'Ow, Ow! Okay! Stop, stop I am hit! *Merde!*'

Yes! He pumped his fist. Claude grumbled and muttered to himself in French as he clambered down. Ocean tried to work out who else was left. He'd seen Kaya, Drew and Claude get hit, which meant the remaining player had to be either Dante or Vasile. Amazing! He was only going to win the bloody thing on his first night.

Claude landed deftly and brushed himself down. 'Good shot.'

Ocean smiled. 'Why thank you squire.'

'You have played very well. It's a shame you didn't win.'

'What do you mean? I'm on fire!'

'Non,' Claude's smile broke into a laugh, '*mon dieu,*' and pointed.

A shiver ran down his spine. Someone was behind him pointing a gun at him, he was sure of it. But when he turned he was shocked to see Vasile's face, upside down.

'What the?'

Vasile grinned and held up a flag. Ocean's hand shot to his back and only grasped air.

'Damn it!'

Like a circus acrobat, Vasile pulled himself up and Ocean saw how he'd done it. The spindly Romanian had slithered along the branch and dangled down with his legs. Anger disintegrated into admiration. The stealth. How on earth had he been able to pull that off?

Rather than clamber down as Claude had, Vasile launched himself from the branch, performed a somersault and landed deftly on his feet.

'Wow!' Ocean held out his hand. 'Congratulations.'

Vasile took it. 'Thank you. I congratulate you too.'

'Why's that?'

Claude clapped him on the back. 'Before you arrived we all predicted you would finish last!'

# 8

# DÉJÀ VU

D espite only having a few hours' sleep, Ocean was still buzzing from the game the night before. He'd played plenty of sports before, paintball included, but last night was edgier somehow—and not only because it was at night. The equipment was incredible and they'd all played to win: Claude hiding up in that tree for hours, Drew's ambush and Vasile's incredible stealth. The whole thing had been amazing.

He met the cook, Sue, in the kitchen. She reminded him of a school dinner lady.

'Alright dearie?' her Leicester accent dragged like baggage. 'Carry this through for me, would you?'

Ocean transported a tray of juices, glasses and cutlery to the table. A basket of boiled eggs, wholegrain bread, fruit salad, muesli and yoghurt were already waiting there. He liked to eat healthily and this struck him as a good sign for the meals to come.

Over breakfast all talk centred on last night's game and a post-mortem on their individual failings, interspersed with observations from Warren. Dante, who had come last, shook his head. '*Madre mía.* I gotta do better that that. Ten minutes in the arena, that's useless.'

Ocean waited. Nobody said anything. Just stony silence. It would fall to him then. 'Don't worry about it man, it was just a game.'

Dante sent him a smile and Ocean was glad he had spoken up, for the little it was worth. After breakfast, the students congregated in the lounge for an introductory meeting with Frank.

'It's our first official day of school here at Hinckley. Each of you is already elite and is here on the recommendation of one our tutors, or myself. There's a deal we need to make here, in this room, before we start in earnest.

'On our side of this agreement, you'll find the facilities are first rate, the tutors the best in their respective fields and we promise you a modest wage during your study here. The astute among you may already have wondered what the catch is with such a sweet deal, and kudos to you for thinking as such, because here's the rub. We expect you to work your asses off, to stretch yourselves beyond what you deem comfortable and trust the experts,' he motioned to the staff, 'beyond what you would normally classify as reasonable. And if you can't fulfil this obligation, then your stay with us will be cut short.'

Ocean imagined himself as unmoulded clay that could be anything if placed in the right sculptor's hands.

'How works this then?' Vasile asked in his bruised English.

'Classes broadly fit into three fields: the physical, the psychological and the technical. Over the next two weeks you'll have classes in all three disciplines with practice tests so you get a measure on your own progress relative to your peers.

Then after those two weeks we will run formal pass/fail tests in all three disciplines. You must pass all three to stay for the summer. Fail and you go home early.'

An uneasy murmur went around the table. Ocean sighed. More tests then. No sooner had he done his GCSEs, the next set would be upon him in two weeks. Then there would be his driving test, perhaps A-Levels and then university maybe. Perhaps it would never end; life would just be a series of tests. It was a depressing thought.

But Uncle Frank wasn't done. 'So, in terms of your practice tests, last night's game of Last One Standing would be in the physical discipline and is scored as follows: Vasile gets one point for finishing first, Ocean two and so on until we get to Dante who gets six. We'll keep a running total. The lower your score, the better you are performing relative to your peers.'

'Wait, so last night counted?' asked Dante.

'These scores are for you to see how you are progressing relative to other students, so you know what you need to work on. The tests that really count will be in two weeks' time.' Uncle Frank replied.

Dante didn't look happy about it.

The first lesson was technical and suddenly took on a new significance. Ocean's place was at stake now, but pressure was often a good motivator in his experience. The lesson took place with Warren in a windowless room in the middle of the farmhouse with three different access doors. Behind these doors, there would no doubt be flashing lights, humming machines, wires and servers to make all the kit work. There was a bank of classy looking computers, chrome flat screens and an interactive white board at the front. Frank was right, no expense had been spared; be it night vision goggles or computers. No wonder there was only six students.

Warren's teaching style was fast-paced and assumed that a competent programming capability was already in place. This was a problem. Ocean had learnt a bit at school and had messed around building that *Rocky* fan site a few years back, but that was about it. Half the problem was understanding what was actually being asked. The language was so technical: shellcode, executable programs, exploits, botnets, malware and buffer overflows. He had to keep a window open to Google the terms and check out what they meant. When he did know what to do, he was glacially slow in working through the problem, barely finishing any but the most simple of tasks. Sitting next to Dante only highlighted, made bold and underlined his inadequacy; the guy was so fast it was a wonder sparks didn't fly off the keyboard. The other students didn't seem to have the same trouble as Ocean. It wasn't just that he couldn't keep the peloton in sight; it was more that he couldn't even mount the bike to pedal and even try.

Warren finished the class with the excellent news that next class, there'd be a practice test. Over a lunch of red pepper and tomato soup, Ocean mindlessly transported the spoon from bowl to mouth. His frazzled mind brimmed with new knowledge he could barely grasp, let alone employ. He tried to recall a string of code Warren had briefly flashed up on the white board that had something to do with buffering or something and he could remember how it started but—

'Hey, don't overthink it.' Dante's voice was low, he gestured with his spoon. 'I can help you if you're worried.'

Ocean stirred the soup, was it that obvious? He thought one of his strengths was hiding his weaknesses. 'Think I'll be alright thanks.'

Dante shrugged. 'As you want.'

After lunch, he checked in with Mum. Yes, he was eating well thanks, and yes, it did include vegetables. Yes, the other kids were fine. Yes, the owners were treating him well. Yes, he was enjoying it. Yes, he'd call again tomorrow, and yes, he loved her too.

The afternoon lesson was physical and would be followed by another practice test. Ocean went out early to try and clear his thoughts from the muddle of code that now caterpillared around his brain. Fields and fields of grassy land were interrupted by contained copses similar to one where they'd played Last One Standing. Leicester was only a half-hour drive away, but this remote place still felt a world away from the constrained huddled terraces on Shoreham beach.

A Land Rover rolled up the drive and came to a stop outside the farmhouse. A lean, muscled man in vest and camo trousers stepped out. His hair was grey, short and spiky. He looked at Ocean and down at his watch.

'You're early.'

'And you're Uri?'

'I am.' Uri had a cockney accent. With a name like Uri, Ocean had expected Russian or Polish or something. Uri opened the boot and started unloading boxes of bike helmets.

'Give me a hand then fella.'

'My name's Ocean.'

Uri smirked. 'And that's your real name?'

Ocean was halfway through conjuring a wisecrack about Uri being short for urine but then thought better of it. 'Yep, Ocean's my real name.'

'Tough break fella.'

'Not really. I like it. It's what they call character building. Suitable only for mockery or greatness, nothing in between.'

Uri squinted at him appraisingly and Ocean was smacked by a sudden *déjà vu*, like maybe he'd seen Uri before from somewhere.

'Let's hope it's greatness and not mockery then shall we?'

Ocean nodded, mind reaching for where he might have seen this man before. 'Uri, you've not been on TV have you?'

Uri ran his hand from jaw to greying crew cut. 'You think I got what it takes to be a star, fella?'

'No,' Ocean laughed, 'it's just I think I might recognise you. God knows from where though.'

'Think I'd remember if I'd met a lad with a name like yours. Ah, here come the others.'

Dante joined him and helped unbox the helmets, finding suitable sizes for everyone while Drew and the others got out the quad bikes. Uri fired them up one by one and Ocean hopped onto his. The engine thrummed beneath his thighs; his hands juddered on the handlebars. Exhaust fumes. Heat. Power. He couldn't wait to open it up. First, he had to endure Uri explaining the controls like they were a bunch of simpletons. He even made them demonstrate they could safely brake and turn about five times even though everyone had gotten it immediately. But then, the wait was over.

Ocean was zipping over the Leicestershire fields whooping into his helmet, grass and dust spraying from behind the wheels. He knew then that he had made the right call about summer; Hinckley farm was nothing short of awesome.

After a few laps of the grounds, Uri made them line up in the middle of a field and cut their engines. Everyone flipped their visors up and all Ocean could see were smile lines.

'That was amazing!'

'Whoo-ey! Let's go again!' yelled Drew.

'Alright morons, calm down,' Uri hopped off his bike and held his helmet under the crook of his arm. He looked at the sky, then down at his watch and nodded to himself. 'Let's give you your next practice test.'

# 9

# QUAD RACE

Ocean hugged his knees tight to the machine and leant into the corner, rounded a stack of old rubber tyres, straightened up and hit the throttle too early. The back wheels snaked, found purchase in the mud and he was off again, hot in pursuit of Kaya and Drew a few seconds ahead.

Out of the periphery of his tinted visor, he caught Claude trying to overtake on the outside.

'*On y va!*' Claude yelled over the drone of the engine.

Ocean gritted his teeth. 'No you don't.' Already at full throttle, he steered wide, forcing Claude even wider and then cut in sharply for the next corner, two bike lengths clear now.

'*Merde!*'

The defence cost him time. Ahead, the woods swallowed Drew up like a black hole. Ocean tore after him, flipping up his visor to adjust to the darker light and slalomed round the first set of trees. The tyres bounced off tree roots and stones, juddering his vision and shaking his grip, he barely clung on to the handlebars. He braked late and just managed to pull the quad bike through a hairpin. He took off again and scissored through the next set of trees. The woodland reverberated with revving engines, crunching tires and dancing lights.

Drew's bike came into view. He was righting his line after what must have been a skid or a bad corner. It was his chance. He nudged his bike alongside, Drew's, wheel to wheel. The woodland track was running out, there was only room for one bike. He edged a nose length ahead—then tipped left.

'Wha—' he couldn't hold it and slipped from his seat. The world spun round and round until he hit the ground with a crunch. His arm jarred painfully. It took a second to realise that he was lying at the bottom of a trench by the track. Brambles enveloped his ankles and thighs. His pain gave way to anger. Drew had pushed him off!

'You cheating, dirty...!'

He got to his feet, tore himself free of the brambles, ignoring the pain and scrambled up the bank. Claude shot by, whooping. Ocean's bike rolled slowly down the side of the track, he hobble-ran after it and leapt on from the back and in the same movement jammed his wrist around the throttle. His bike accelerated, spitting him out of the woods. He had to get back in the race.

'Come on!' he careened across the field at full speed, following Claude's line. Drew's bike was a speck in the distance. He checked behind; Dante was fending off Vasile. Little danger of being caught. Ocean leant as far as he dared for a long sweeping bend, hitting the apex. He closed in on Claude, choking down more exhaust smoke and getting spattered with grass. He tipped down his visor and crouched low, pulling in tight behind Claude for the straight. He edged dangerously close to the back of Claude's bike, got in the slipstream and eased off the throttle, finding he could still keep pace with the Frenchman. He was close enough to see his own lights reflecting on the back of Claude's helmet, too close … As the final corner approached, he made his move.

He pulled to the outside, increased the throttle and drew alongside Claude.

'Ha! Good try!' Claude yelled, letting his bike drift wider to cut him off—the same move Ocean had done to him earlier. Ocean cut the throttle, enough to send Claude past and darted back to take the inside line with a yank of the steering column and maxing the acceleration. The bike lurched but responded perfectly. When he took the corner he wasn't quite level with Claude, but he had the line and inched into the lead.

'Come on, come on.' Still at full throttle, he dodged every few seconds to block Claude from slipstreaming him back.

He crossed the line and made a beeline straight for Drew and Kaya, who were sitting casually on their bikes with their helmets off, chatting to Uri like they'd been done for an hour. Ocean leapt off his bike and threw his helmet to the ground.

'What the hell was that?'

Kaya and Drew looked at each other and shrugged. He fronted up to Drew and shoved him as hard as he could.

'Oi!' Uri snapped. 'Calm it you!'

Drew was built like a buffalo and kept his footing easily. The American went an angry red, took two quick steps and boom, shoved Ocean back twice as hard. Ocean, barely kept his feet, but he wasn't through.

'What's your problem man?' Drew spat.

'My problem? What? Do you not remember pushing me into a ditch?'

He waited for Drew to deny it, a denial that would earn him the gift of knuckles to the face. He didn't care how big the guy was.

'Yeah, I pushed you off. So what?'

Ocean couldn't believe what he was hearing. 'What? You actually think it's okay to do that? I could've broken my neck!'

Uri moved between them. 'I'm calm,' he said softly, 'and you two better join me sharpish because you don't want to see what I'm like when I'm pissed off.'

Ocean appealed to him. 'But he pushed me off my bike!'

Uri fixed him a hard stare. 'Stop whining child. You were beaten. Deal with it like a man.'

Ocean blushed with embarrassment, only making Drew smirk all the more.

'Real winners do whatever it takes to win. There's no dirty, no unfair and that's the black and white facts of it. Winner,' Drew pointed to himself, 'and loser,' he pointed to Ocean.

'Actually meathead,' Kaya chipped in, '*I'm* the winner here. You came second.'

'Shut it!' Uri raised his voice now. 'Go on, back to the house and stop acting up.'

Claude grabbed his shoulder. 'Come on man, let's cool off.'

Ocean let himself be led. 'What a nob.'

'Drew or Uri?'

'Both of them.'

Belatedly, Dante came over the line, followed by Vasile.

Dante palmed up his visor. 'Who won?'

'Kaya,' Claude replied.

'Come on Dante,' Ocean said. 'Head back with us.'

Ocean tried to push the incident with Drew out of his mind; with the coding test on the horizon and his place at the school on the line, he didn't want to waste energy bearing grudges.

## ORCA RISING

Scarlet's first lesson was on social dynamics. She played video footage of a group of lawyers out for lunch and asked the students to estimate each individual's status based on their body language and appearance. The alpha was fairly obvious, holding court and pointing with his fork as he talked. The influencer was quiet and thoughtful in an expensive suit. When he spoke, even the alpha sat back and listened. The two junior lawyers were the lambs, always seeking approval. One assumed a higher social status as he could make the alpha laugh more often. It made Ocean think about their own group at Hinckley … what was he? A bit of them all it seemed.

Scarlet's next class was a deeper look into Non-Verbal Communication or NVC, and Appearance Reading. Ocean knew a bit about NVC already, like how touching your face can mean you're lying, or crossing your legs towards somebody is a sign of attraction. But there were also things Ocean hadn't thought to read into before; checking the most worn holes on a belt might tell you if that person had lost or put on weight recently. Tan lines; cologne; choice of phone; their handshake; their walk even. So much. It was like he'd been walking around half-blind until now.

'The signs are all there, waiting to be read, interpreted and used to your advantage.' Scarlet would say periodically, or something akin. Soon, she claimed, the students would be able to manipulate their own NVC and appearance in order to assume different social roles within a group dynamic.

Ocean couldn't believe they didn't teach that sort of thing at normal school. Surely understanding people, their desires and motivations would be helpful in any line of work? Warren's classes, on the other hand, remained tough. The first week covered basic encryption and decryption. The coding however, was turning into a major problem for him. Warren ran two practice tests that first week and Ocean came last in both. It just wasn't like him, to be the worst at something and he hated it ... but he just didn't have the knack. It was unnatural to sit in front of a screen for hours on end and he couldn't bring himself to revise all he'd learnt. Coding was just like sprouts. He'd push them to the edge of his plate for as long as he could. But sooner or later he'd have to eat them.

The other practice tests weren't an issue. In Scarlet's test he managed to separate lies from truth when watching some staged video footage. The physical tests were going well—he even picked up his first win in the distance run. The problem was the technical. When he looked at the scores on the board, he was now in second last place, only ahead of Dante. Uncle Frank had said that they needed to pass all three tests to stay. And now he was learning so much, he couldn't leave. Drastic action was needed. It was time to eat the sprouts.

He found Dante in the kitchen, helping himself to a bag of crisps.

'Put down the bag and step away from the crisps. Repeat, step away from the crisps.'

Dante shrugged, popped another in his mouth. 'Salt & Vinegar, we don't have these flavours in Spain. So good.'

'I think we can help each another. If you accept, it'll mean no crisps for a while.'

# 10

# LIE

They started the next day. Ocean dragged Dante out of bed at 6am. It was a crisp morning, the sun peeking its nose over the horizon. Still groggy from sleep, Ocean led them through some stretches in silence. Soon enough, he was bright and alert, blood pumping around his body as he set the pace. Birds burst from hedgerows at their thudding feet. Dante breathed heavily, but didn't complain. It didn't take a class in NVC with Scarlet to work out that Dante was determined. Ocean pushed until his own lungs burnt.

'Come on, you can do it!' he called over his shoulder.

Back at the farmhouse, drenched in sweat, Ocean logged the run as forty-eight minutes. He'd normally clock 10k in thirty-nine minutes on a very average day, but it was a start. All Dante had to do was show willing, work hard and the times would drop. Maybe lady luck would grant Ocean the same deal with the technical.

Ocean made them a breakfast of porridge and tea. The radio was on:

'Coming up: An interview with British tennis sensation Max Harper who is in action next week at Queens as he warms up for Wimbledon—'

Ocean cut it with a twist.

Dante grunted. 'The Spanish are the best at tennis.'

'Glad I'm not at home. Mum uses Queens as a warm up for tennis party season. By the time Wimbledon comes along it's unbearable. It's just an excuse to see who can drink the most Pimms and eat the most bowlfuls of strawberries and cream without throwing up.'

'Sounds gross.'

It was. But perhaps this year would be more sedate after self-banned Andy's tennis club punching incident. All the same, he was glad that he didn't have to suffer through it this year. Unless he didn't make it through the technical test of course ... He supped at his mug of tea too fast, burning his mouth.

'Come on Dante, let's get onto this coding practice.'

The week that followed was a bit of a blur. Ocean's favourite parts of the *Rocky* series were the montage scenes where Rocky pounds his fists into hunks of frozen meat, runs up steps, roads and mountains all to that iconic theme music. Ocean started to see his own week working with Dante in its own cinematic way.

Sneaking out at the crack of dawn for their run; feet pounding through mud and rain, sweat staining Dante's grey hoody; Ocean reading a textbook and Dante leaning over his shoulder pointing out something on the page; Ocean pushing the pace, yelling encouragement from behind, giving Dante a shove whenever he slowed down; Ocean flying into a frustrated rage and throwing the book against the wall, Dante picking it up again and taking Ocean through it again; Ocean waiting for Dante to run the last few yards, hitting a button on a stopwatch and frowning at the forty-six minutes fifteen seconds time; Ocean calling Mum, checking in; Ocean slapping

Dante on the back; Dante leaning on his knees, puking; Ocean coming last in the next technical practice test, but not so far behind the others as before; in Scarlet's class, the students all looking up at the screen where a man sits a polygraph on camera; the boys running abreast in T-shirts, laughing in the morning air; a close up on the stopwatch—forty-four minutes, forty-two seconds, Ocean nodding to himself; Dante standing cross-armed behind Ocean tapping away at a computer and shaking his head; Ocean biting his tongue in concentration as he finishes a line of code, hits return, pumps his hands in the air in celebration and high-fives Dante; the stopwatch reading forty-three minutes, fifty-one seconds; Ocean calling Mum, checking in; Dante and Ocean doing chin-ups on a branch in the woods; Ocean's fingers dancing over the keyboard, lines of code breeding on the screen before his eyes; Dante and Ocean sprinting the last few yards, racing against each other; forty-one minutes and three seconds. Ocean finishing fifth on the next technical practice test, ahead of Vasile.

By the time the first pass/fail test got called, there was a nervous buzz of excitement amongst the students. Scarlet asked them to wait in the lounge. Ocean sat with Dante and Claude.

'Do you think we've been focussing too much on the physical and the technical? We've hardly done a thing on the psychological stuff.' Dante said.

'Jesus, don't say that now! It's too late to do anything about it! Anyway, how can you prepare for Scarlet's stuff?'

'You could meditate, do some Buddhist chanting perhaps,' said Claude, but Ocean was too nervous to laugh.

'What do you think it will be?'

Dante shrugged. 'Appearance reading maybe.'

'Spotting lies,' suggested Claude. Both sounded plausible.

Scarlet stepped into the lounge and all went quiet.

'Morning everyone.'

'Morning Scarlet.'

'Thanks for waiting. As you know you've got your psychological test this morning. It is pass/fail. Like the physical and technical tests, your place at Hinckley rests on your success, so good luck.' She paused. 'I'll ask each of you in turn to come to an interview room with me where I will ask you five straightforward questions. You must answer each of these questions with a lie. You will be hooked up to a polygraph, a lie-detecting machine, which monitors a range of internal responses: your pulse rate, breathing patterns, blood pressure and perspiration. To pass, you must cheat the machine and stop it from detecting at least one of your five lies.'

Jaws fell open around the room, Ocean's included. A lie-detector test?

Claude shook his head. 'Pardon my French but we in the *merde*.'

'*Ay, por dios,*' said Dante.

'Keep calm,' Ocean said, though he didn't feel it. 'Maybe this is part of it, you know, putting us on edge before we go in.'

Scarlet cleared her throat. 'Ocean? You're first.'

His calm detonated.

Dante's fingernails sunk into his arm. 'Keep calm, focus!'

'You can do this,' said Claude.

It was a small, oppressive room: a desk, two chairs and a small window overlooking the drive outside. Ocean eyed the tangle of equipment warily while Scarlet hooked up two sensors onto his fingers and strapped two others to his arm.

67

'It's like being on life support,' he grimaced. As if appearing carefree enough to joke could hide his nerves.

'Relax. I'll ask you two practice questions. Answer the first truthfully, the second with a lie. Then the examination will begin. Good luck.'

He closed his eyes and tried to loosen the tautness below his neck.

'Is your name Ocean Daley?'

'Yes,' he replied.

Scarlet looked over her glasses at her laptop. 'That's fine, try to focus on something calming, that was fairly close to the limit.'

God, if he couldn't get a correct reading for the truth how was he going to manage a machine-beating lie?

'Are you sixteen years old?'

'No.'

'Very good. That registered as a clear lie. Ready?'

'Yep.'

Scarlet glanced at the screen. The edge of her mouth curled in a grin. 'We won't count that as one of the five, shall we?'

Bloody hell. He was going home. He didn't stand a chance. He thought of all he and Dante had done that week, how hard they'd worked and how little sleep they'd gotten in their quest for improvement. But no, he wouldn't go down without a fight. Rocky knew that, you keep moving forward no matter what ... except, how do you fight when your opponent is yourself?

'Did you take your GCSE's this summer Ocean?'

*Breathe. Come on.* Steady and even, but no. Blood hurtled round his body like a Ferris wheel caught in a hurricane.

68

'No.' Instant failure. *Come on. Just one, that's all I need.*

'Your father was Jack Daley?'

He thought of those movie nights, his feet resting on his father's lap. 'No.'

The harder he tried to control himself the shorter became his breath, the more the sweat prickled his brow. This wasn't working.

'Do you speak Hungarian?'

'Yes,' he replied quickly, perhaps speed would stop his mind from overthinking it. Scarlet's face was implacable but the spiky graphs reflected back in her glasses.

'Do you have fourteen toes?'

He took a breath. Tried to imagine a place, any place. Where did he feel most calm and relaxed?

'Yes.'

A small grimace appeared on Scarlet's face. One last chance. He closed his eyes. Emptied his mind. Blue. A beige speck; a body floating face up to the sky. It was him. Limbs weightless, gently tugged this way and that by the tendril currents suffused within this mass of sea. There was nothing to hold on to here, no control and no illusion of it, only the whim of nature. Above, there was the plane in the sky, looping amongst the clouds.

'... you married with two children?'

He barely sensed the question; it was like music heard underwater.

'Yes,' he exhaled.

# 11

# LUCIFER'S MUD RUN

Ocean waited up in the dorm. Claude entered; his grin wide.

'You did it?'

'*Oui!* I don't know how, but who cares!'

'Me too, the very last question.'

'How do you think Dante will do?'

'I don't know. I just hope he makes it.'

'Me too.'

They didn't have to wait long. Dante peered round the door and blew out his cheeks.

'Well?' asked Ocean and Claude simultaneously.

'Sorry *chicos*,' he shook his head and stuffed his hands in his pockets. 'I just didn't know how to beat that thing. Tell me you made it at least?'

Ocean nodded mechanically. The relief at passing was now riddled with disappointment. All that work Dante had put in counted for nothing now. Dante would have had a good chance of passing the physical and would have aced the technical. What a waste.

'Bollocks!' Ocean punched the mattress.

Dante laughed and pointed at them.

*'Qu-est-ce que c'est?'*

'You fools, I'm a player. Of course I passed.'

Ocean jumped up and play-punched him lightly on the arm. 'You bloody liar!'

'I got two past the machine. I think she must have that thing set to easy for us or something, no way we could all pass it.'

What did it matter? They were through. He smacked Dante on the back. 'Get through the physical and you're on the home straight.'

If only he could say the same for himself.

The physical was that very afternoon. To Ocean's astonishment, all the students had passed the psychological; Dante must have been right about the machine's parameters. The students crowded onto a hired minibus with Uri. As the bus rumbled across the Midlands, Ocean still couldn't shake the sensation that he'd seen Uri before. Despite stealing glances at him in the rear-view mirror, he still couldn't place him.

'Ocean, what's that?' Kaya asked, pointing out the window. 'It's a banner. A sign. For something called *Lucifer's Mud Run. One mile away.'*

Ocean shrugged. 'How would I know?'

'Well, you're the only English one here so I thought you might have heard of it?'

'Yeah come on Fish n' Chips,' said Drew, 'be useful for once.'

'It's an assault course, you morons,' said Uri. 'Six kilometres of mud, obstacles and pain. The owner owes me a favour and he's happy to have a few test rats run it before the public event next week. All obstacles, the whole circuit in thirty minutes. Not a second longer. Failure to do so will mean expulsion from our school,' Uri couldn't hide the sadistic pleasure in his voice, 'I've been looking forward to this for days!'

The six students lined up. Ocean did some stretches. 6k in thirty minutes. If it was a straight run that would be easy, it just depended on the obstacles. Some deep breaths to increase the oxygen flow. Beside him, Dante took a sip of water and stared wild-eyed at the course in front of him.

'If I fall back, don't wait for me *tío*.'

'Don't talk like that. You're ready for this, come on, get fired up, let's destroy it!'

Dante bounced on his toes and shook out his hands. 'You're right. *Vamos tío!*'

'Ready!' Uri yelled from a loudspeaker. 'Three, two, one, go!'

Ocean kept pace with Dante, jogging the first two hundred metres whilst the other four sprinted ahead, Kaya quickly taking the lead. Dante started to speed up.

'Hold your pace,' Ocean said between breaths. 'Conserve energy.'

The first obstacle was an eight-foot high wooden wall. The other students were scrabbling against it, unable to reach the top. In Shoreham his basketball buddies used to have competitions to see who would be the first to dunk the ball in the net. Some had bought special shoes whilst others hit the gym to work on leg presses to build their spring. Ocean did both but reckoned his success was ninety per cent technique and ten per cent shoes. The wall was lower than a basketball net, but he was in normal trainers, not his pumps. He sprinted a few steps ahead of Dante, planted his foot in the middle of the wall and used the grip to propel himself high enough to reach the beam at the top. He pulled himself up, straddled the wall and turned to pull Dante up. But Dante was already up, straddling the wall too, having copied Ocean's method.

'Ocean!' Claude looked up pleadingly. Ocean offered down a hand and pulled him up instead.

'*Merci.*'

'Hey me too!' yelled Drew. Ocean grinned, gave him the finger and slipped down onto the other side. God that felt good.

Ocean, Dante and Claude ran on, crawling under cargo nets into a bog, then, covered in gloopy mud, hurdling over straw bales wrapped in barbed wire. At the side of the course, plumes of flame shot up sporadically. It was like the set of some action movie, sprinting over obstacles with the glow of fire on their muddy faces.

'They're gaining on us.' Dante's breath was laboured.

Ocean glanced back. Kaya was skipping over the hurdles like a pro, and further behind was Drew, moving with surprising fluidity for such a big guy; like watching logs slip through rapids.

'We gotta beat the clock, not them. Focus on our race.'

Despite his words he couldn't remember seeing Vasile. That wasn't good. They reached a tea-coloured pond with monkey bars hanging over. Claude went first. Ocean gave him two-rung head start and followed. The rungs were slippery and cold. Dante grunted with effort behind. Then, a splash. Ocean swung around and saw Dante spitting the brown water out of his mouth in the pond below.

Dante started to swim for the other side.

'No, go back! Do it again, don't give them an excuse to disqualify you.'

'It's too slippery!'

'Do it!' Ocean climbed back the way he came, his arms burning at their sockets.

Dante was dripping wet, panting with his hands on his knees. 'I can't do it.'

'Take off your shirt and wrap it around your hand, it'll give you more grip.'

Ocean took off his own shirt. 'Put this around your other hand.'

Kaya shot past them and deftly clambered across. She was light. Ocean wondered how Drew would fare. On the other side, Claude hadn't waited. That was fair enough, he supposed.

'Breathe! Go first, I'll be right behind.'

Then Drew appeared, barging them both out the way, then double taking at their bare chests. 'Ha! Fitting in some time for romance guys?' and took the bars two at a time with his big gorilla arms.

Ocean shoved Dante. 'Go!'

With his hands wrapped in the T-shirts, Dante moved slowly but steadily across the bars. Ocean's own arms burnt like fire but he couldn't let on, he needed Dante to focus on himself. One rung at a time.

They made it across. Relief flooded through Ocean's arms and shoulders.

'*Gracias tío,*' Dante threw him back his shirt.

Ocean started running, putting it on as he went. 'Come on, we need to make back some time.'

Ocean pushed. Then he caught sight of Drew, but even at a good pace he couldn't seem to reel him in. He'd thought Drew was just a strength guy, but he apparently had a high fitness level too. Damn him.

Ocean checked his watch. Twenty-seven minutes and he couldn't see any finish line. 'Come on, we must nearly be there, one last push.' He put on a spurt to the top of an incline and caught his breath on the hilltop, calves stinging. There was a zip wire going down some two hundred metres into a small lake. Drew was front crawling from the middle to the edge, and there, another hundred metres or so from the bank was the finish line.

'Come on! *Vamos* Dante! I can see the line!'

Ocean descended the last few steps to pull Dante up and pushed him over to the zip wire. He checked the watch. Twenty-eight minutes twenty seconds. Not two minutes to go.

'Hold on tight, catch your breath on the zip down and then swim like buggery for the shore.' He wrapped Dante's hands around the handles. 'Go!'

Ocean grabbed the next set. Dante was halfway down, so Ocean launched off. He lifted his legs for extra speed, air buffeting his hair and skin. Twenty-nine minutes and four seconds. Dante hit the water and his arms beat a frenzied but ineffective front crawl towards the shore. There was nothing more Ocean could do for him now. Ocean hoisted himself up on the zip and replaced his hands with his feet so he was hanging upside down. He craned his neck. The water rushed towards him, he swung back and forth, freeing his feet and perfected a dive straight into the water. He kept his body packed in tight and his hands outstretched underwater and wriggled his body in a fluid, seal-like stroke. He went some twenty metres and unsure of his direction in the murky water, came up. He was nearly at the bank. Dante was scrambling out the lake.

'Go!'

## ORCA RISING

A few powerful strokes of front crawl brought Ocean to the shore, the last few water dragging steps were painfully slow. The watch. Twenty-nine minutes and forty seconds. They weren't going to make it.

He sprinted, powering his feet into the slippery mud and pumping his knees. How far was it, 120 metres? 150? It looked further from down here. His breath felt like it was coming out of his ears. His lungs burnt, he had mud in his right eye making it hard to see clearly. Dante was ahead, staggering for the finish; Claude was on the line, hands cupped around his mouth yelling something; Uri was holding a stopwatch; Kaya and Drew were finished too, cross armed and bored.

He pumped his legs desperate to go faster, to find that bit extra. Dante was a few yards from the line, blocking Ocean's trajectory. He couldn't go around, there just wasn't time. With whatever he had left in the tank, Ocean roared, leant his weight forward for extra momentum, feet whirling in the mud like a cartoon character and propelled himself headfirst. Then he did the only thing he could.

He dived for the line as if Dante wasn't there.

In part-rugby tackle, part-battering ram he slammed into Dante, shooting forwards, skidding through the sloppy mud and over the line.

'Urgh.' Dante groaned.

Ocean rolled onto his back, gasped air by the greedy lungful and searched for Uri. He was staring at the stopwatch and he didn't look happy.

'Did ... we ... make it?'

Uri shook his head, 'Un-be-fecking-lievable, 'he held out the watch. It read twenty-nine minutes, fifty-nine seconds and three tenths. 'You are the flukiest morons on the face of this planet.'

There was a splash and they all turned to see Vasile desperately swimming to the shore.

'Too late loser!' Drew yelled.

Ocean didn't have enough strength to feel any pity for Vasile or any joy for himself. All he could do was lie prostrate on the mud next to Dante. Drew leant over them and for a second Ocean wondered if he might offer a hand to pull him up, but no, he was smirking instead.

'You two fellas just can't get enough of each other can you? The mud make you horny or something?'

Kaya nudged Drew. 'Wow Drew, nice outlook, where did you get that, the nineties?'

'I passed them halfway round and they were topless!'

Kaya shrugged. 'I think it's sweet.'

At that exact moment, Dante rolled to one side and puked his guts out into the mud. Very sweet indeed.

# 12

## URI

A taxi came to pick up Vasile from the farmhouse in plenty of time to catch his flight home to Bucharest. Ocean shook Vasile's hand, wishing he'd made more of an effort to get to know the guy better. He'd been incredible at their game of Last One Standing and maybe would have passed the physical with some help. But most of all, Ocean was just glad that the taxi wasn't his ... though perhaps the next one would be. The technical loomed like a monster in his mind.

As a type of reward, or perhaps to give Sue the night off, the students chose from an Indian takeaway menu for dinner that evening. Uri was left in charge and phoned in the order.

'I'll do a run on the bike, be twenty minutes or so,' Uri picked up his leather jacket.

'Awesome, thanks dude,' Drew said.

Uri shot him a withering look. 'Don't call me that, ever.'

It was a chill evening for summer and Claude lit the fire. Ocean didn't want to hang around too long; he wanted to go over all he'd learnt with Dante on encryption, coding and protection for tomorrow's test. With his achy limbs and tired body, coding revision was the last thing he felt like doing but that's how it was with sprouts. You couldn't keep pushing them to the edge of the plate.

Kaya was sprawled on the sofa, blanket over her legs, the crackling fire catching her glossy hair in the light. She'd finished Lucifer's Mud Run first. Ocean had never known a girl like her; she was so strong, unflappable and as beautiful as she was unapproachable. She yawned and rested her head to one side and for a flicker of a moment he suddenly wished she were leaning on him. 'I wonder if we'll all make it through tomorrow's technical,' she yawned.

Drew snorted. 'Ocean won't, that's for sure. Hey Ocean, have you even heard of the Internet? You should really head to the library and look up some information about it in a book, I hear it's going to be huge.'

Like a boxer in the ninth, Ocean still had enough energy left for a tired swipe back. 'I'm sure you know all about huge, seeing as you're such a massive tool.'

'Snap!' Kaya laughed.

But Drew grinned and made a show of adjusting his crotch. 'Yeah I know *all* about massive.'

'*El fuego,*' Dante pointed, in what was a very deliberate ploy to curb the conversation, 'put more wood on there would you Ocean?'

Ocean stoked the fire half-heartedly. Added a log. Maybe he should just skip dinner altogether and hit the books … or the screens or whatever. The motorbike growled in the yard, Uri was back. That settled it. He'd eat, get his energy up and pull a late one with Dante. He dusted his hands. 'I'll see if Uri needs any help.'

'Suck-up,' Drew crooned.

Ocean padded into the hall, rubbing his aching limbs and got the door.

'Need a hand?'

Uri's, helmet tucked under his arm, stamped his feet a couple of times on the mat.

And that was it. Ocean froze. He knew where he'd seen Uri before.

'Look lively.' Uri's helmet sailed towards him, but his reactions were slow, blunted by shock. It landed with a crack on the floor.

'Oi, butterfingers, that better not be damaged or you'll be buying a new one.'

'Sorry ... I.' He suddenly didn't know how to act.

'What's up with you fella? You don't look so good.'

'Nothing. Just tired.' Ocean examined the helmet. 'No harm done. Look.'

Uri swung a backpack from shoulder to floor. 'Food's all in here, lay it out on the table. There's a couple of beers in the side pocket, stick them in the fridge for me.'

'Sure.' Ocean reached for the rucksack but Uri grabbed his arm.

'Something is up, isn't it?'

Ocean shook his arm away. 'Nothing.' He took the backpack to the kitchen, glad to escape Uri's scrutiny. What did it mean? The fridge hummed its soothingly undertone. Open. Yellow light reached out, embalming his flushed face with a cool blast of air. Why would Uri pretend not to know him? It had only been a few years. He unloaded the beer.

'Why did you just go all bonkers on me fella?' Uri said.

Ocean shut the fridge door. 'What do you mean?'

Uri stepped deeper into the kitchen. 'I'm no mug. Tell me.'

'There's nothing to tell.'

Uri changed from man to blur and before Ocean could even see what was going on, his face was pressed hard against the fridge door, nose squished and arm twisted high up his back. He gasped; the pain was so intense he was sure his arm was about to snap in two.

'Now you listen to me you little punk. I am more dangerous than you could ever know. NEVER lie to me! When I ask you something you bloody well answer!'

'Alright! Alright! I know you!'

The grip loosened and Uri let go. Sweet relief. Ocean massaged the joints and muscles, not meeting Uri's eye.

'Talk. How exactly do you know me?'

Ocean closed his eyes, remembering the day in Shoreham when he had answered the door to a man in military uniform with a cap tucked under his arm.

'You came to our house to tell us Dad had died. And now you're here with Uncle Frank, pretending like you've never seen me before. What's going on?'

'Move,' Uri nudged Ocean out the way, opened the fridge and got out the two bottles of beer, popped the caps with his teeth and handed one to Ocean.

'I want answers, not a beer.'

Uri shook his head, ran his hands through his hair. 'I don't know what to tell you fella.'

'Why?'

'I promised Frank I wouldn't.'

Exasperated, Ocean wanted to hurl the bottle at the window. 'You've got to give me something! My head's imploding right now.'

'I think you'd better speak to Frank.'

'My Dad is he—'

'Yes. I'm sorry, he really did cop it.'

'Then why the—'

'Really fella,' Uri's voice was stern, 'I'm losing my patience here. Just speak to Frank will you?'

The kitchen lights sprung on.

'What are you two losers doing in the dark?' Drew said.

# 13

## SNOOKERED

Uncle Frank's room was on the top floor of the farmhouse. Skylights threw in eerie nocturnal light onto a line of tribal masks hanging upon the corridor wall. Ocean trod warily past them, their dead wooden eyes and anguish-twisted mouths gave him the creeps. Before he could even knock, Uncle Frank's door opened and out his uncle stepped, cutting a strange figure in the doorway with striped pyjamas and his fedora. Did he sleep in that thing? Shower in it?

'I don't like being disturbed,' Uncle Frank said.

'I know.'

'Out with it then.'

Ocean summarised his conversation, or lack of one, with Uri.

Uncle Frank sighed and scooped glasses from around the chain of his neck and placed them on the bridge of his nose and gave Ocean an appraising look with piercing blue eyes. It struck Ocean that this was the first time he'd seen his uncle without sunglasses on.

'If we're having this conversation right now, then we aren't doing it here,' he scratched his beard, 'I'll get my dressing gown.'

Ocean's heart leapt. Finally, some answers.

"Not here," as it turned out, meant a large snooker room at the back of the tutors' sleeping quarters. Uncle Frank switched on a couple of electric heaters and handed Ocean a cue.

'Want to start?'

The heaters clicked and clanged into life.

'I think you'd better start, don't you?'

'Very well,' Uncle Frank bent over the table, pressed his hand to the felt, 'such a beautiful game. The pool obsessed Yanks got this one wrong. Patience, strategy, depth ...' he paused, stroked the white down the table, 'and execution.'

The white nibbled at the edge of the triangle of reds, splitting the pack with a malty kiss and returned to the top of the table an inch or two behind the yellow.

'Such a meditative pursuit. A patient game. Ideal for the type of conversation we need to have.'

Nervous, Ocean lined up a loose, unpottable red. 'And what sort of conversation *are* we about to have?' he hit a passable safety, leaving nothing on for Uncle Frank to pot.

'One that requires patience. You will get some answers but not all. You'll soon understand why.' Uncle Frank gunned the white down the table, swerving it between the blue and the pink and potted a red in the bottom right. An impossible shot. No celebration or satisfaction flickered in his expression. Uncle Frank sighed and squeezed the bridge of his nose between the eyes with his thumb and forefinger.

'Ocean, your dad wasn't really in the army.'

'What?'

'Well, he was for a couple of years before you were born. But that was it. Me and him, we worked together after that.'

Ocean couldn't process this. Too many questions fought for superiority in his muddled brain. 'How the... and Uri? He was in army uniform? My Mum, does she know? And her army pension, what—'

'Ocean, calm it,' Uncle Frank twisted chalk onto the head of his cue and blew dust off. Ocean wanted to wrap his cue around Uncle Frank's head but there would be no rushing him. He was always in control and willing to turn the conversational tap off on a whim. Uncle Frank lined up the black, slotted it in the bottom left.

'The nature of our business relates to the existence of this summer school and your presence here.'

That was a bit vague. Ocean leant his palms on the edge of the table. 'Which is?'

'Not something I can tell you now. Perhaps not ever. It depends on tomorrow. Your final test.'

'This is crazy! So Uri pretending to be in the army and all that stuff about an IED in Afghanistan was all bull?'

'Uri might have been in the army for all you know and this is just the natural progression of his career. And the IED? What does it matter if he died in an explosion or someplace else? Does it alter the fact of it?'

Ocean was stunned for a moment. His uncle even resumed play, potting a red and back spinning to line up the pink for the middle.

'It matters to me how he died.'

'You'd better pass your test tomorrow then Ocean. I'm bound to a code and I won't break it unless you pass initiation.'

'Initiation? Code? What *is* all this Uncle Frank?'

'Look Ocean I'm tired. Tired of kicking your ass at this game too. If you pass tomorrow, you'll learn more.'

'Why won't you tell me anything useful?'

'Secrecy is extremely important for us,' Uncle Frank said with enough menace in his voice that Ocean knew not to push any more. His uncle rolled his cue onto the table, knocking the balls into an untidy line. 'Either forget it, or be patient. We're done here.'

And with that, he was gone.

Ocean resisted the urge to snap the cue over his knee, but it was hard. Why did people who had all the knowledge laud it over everyone else? And his dad too, all those years he'd acted out a lie to his own family. But why? And what was this school for? There was the lie detector test, the appearance reading, the coding as well as the physical trials Uri had put them through. They were being groomed for something. All of them were. The question was, for what?

It was nearly ten o'clock by the time he left the snooker room. Ocean microwaved the curry leftovers and wolfed them down in the kitchen. After, he found Dante snoozing on the couch. He shook his friend awake.

'Urgh, *qué*?' Dante looked this way and that, regaining consciousness. There was a small pool of drool on the cushion where he'd been resting his head.

'I'm sorry man, I know you're shattered. I am too. But I really need your help.'

Dante rubbed his eyes, nodded and sat up. 'Let's go.'

In the computer room, Ocean fired up two machines and was glad for the accompanying hum and noise to fill the silence of the classroom.

'What do you want to cover *tío*?'

'I need to revise for the test tomorrow, but I have an idea … I can do some practice tasks on here and if I get stuck I can ask you a question.'

Dante moved to turn off his machine. 'Okay, so we don't need both.'

'Wait. Seeing as we're here. Maybe you could work your magic for me on something?'

Dante's eyes narrowed. '*Qué?*'

'Do you think you could maybe break into the school system and take a look around?'

'What? Why would I do that?'

'Dante, aren't you suspicious about this place at all? How did you even come to be here anyway?'

'I got a bit of a rep in certain hacking circles in Spain. Warren sought me out and offered me two thousand euros just to meet him for an hour and talk. He pitched this place to me and I thought why not? Worst that can happen is I get some money for my family and see the UK.'

'But aren't you curious about what they want us for? There's got to be something else in it for them right? I keep thinking back to that lie detector test, why is deception suddenly a coveted skill?'

'It's just a stupid test.'

'And the coding? It's decryption, some problem solving tasks that are really more like hacking methodologies when you think about it.'

A faint light went on in Dante's eyes. 'Sort of true.'

'So shall we scratch the itch of our curiosity or what?'

Dante bit his lip, then nodded. 'Okay, nothing risky though. I'll need you to tell me what I'm searching for. It's not a question of just browsing through someone's folders and getting lucky. I'll bet they're employing all sorts of obfuscation techniques.'

And so, Ocean selfishly went about doing practice tasks he thought might be in the test the next day. If he could scrape a pass then he might get some answers, but he wasn't going to miss his only chance to find out more. He was tired of being in the dark, being kept on the back-foot by his uncle.

He'd just done a basic reverse engineering task when Dante leaned over.

'I've got something.'

Ocean bent over the screen. 'What?'

'I tried your uncle's name, the school name, the students ... and that's when I found this.'

On the screen there was a folder titled O.D.

'Open it.'

Dante double clicked, a sub-folder opened with over a dozen files. He opened one at random. It filled the screen with Ocean's SAT results. With open-mouthed amazement, he watched Dante open another with his results from his mocks, a digital copy of his passport, dental records and then, even more bizarrely were pictures of Ocean playing sports for school; one of him dribbling a football down the wing, another mid-rally during a tennis game. There were Excel files with tables of scores and results from the various sports he'd done at school.

'Where the hell did they ...'

'I know! But guess what? There's a file for each of us, here's the one they took from my school in Cádiz.'

'I can't believe how creepily thorough ... wait, is that a first aid certificate?'

'*Dios mío*, they even have my guitar grades. I sucked. Gave up when I was ten.'

'This is so weird.'

'There's more. I found the curriculum.'

It was a grid, no, a timetable. Ocean filleted it. The first part showed the classes they'd done already. Then there was a line break with INITIATION TESTS. Underneath that was an array of lessons that amazed and confused him: Neuro-Linguistic Programming, Surveillance Techniques, System Hijacks, Advanced Bugging, Body Combat, Social Dynamics, Spanish (Warren), Arabic (Uri), Russian (Scarlet), Poisons (and their uses) and another line-break with FIELD MISSIONS.

He looked at Dante. Dante back at him.

'What the hell is this place?'

# 14

# CODING TEST

Exhausted physically and mentally, Ocean and Dante called it a night shortly after one in the morning. Ocean lay in his bunk with Claude fidgeting above him, making the mattress springs groan and wheeze. Nagging thoughts nibbled at the edges of his consciousness, poking him, preventing him from the sleep he desperately craved. There was too much dammed up now: Uri, the weird curriculum, Uncle Frank's evasiveness, the files they'd uncovered about themselves...Something deeply strange was happening at Hinckley Farm. Were he in a sharper frame of mind he might have hypothesised, made some cleaner connections. Was this school leading to something good?

For the defence: his own uncle and his father worked for this organisation and surely that would mean a force for good? But then, for the prosecution: the secrecy, the lie detector test, the curriculum with subjects like "Poisons (and their uses)" and "Advanced Surveillance" hardly sounded like instruments for the benevolent. Hand on heart time. He didn't know Uncle Frank that well ... but how well had he truly known his own father?

He had to break the dam. He had to let the truth flood out. It wasn't patience he needed. He had to pass the technical the next day and play their game for now. And with that determined thought, sleep finally found him.

Ocean prepared as well as he could given the circumstances. He allowed himself to sleep until ten—there was no point going in tired. Feverish cramming, in his experience, did more harm than good. Instead, he lightly went over his notes, talked over some of the trickier points with Dante, ate a good lunch, drank tea and got his head in the zone.

'Remember,' Dante said on their way to the computer room, 'there are often many ways of working through a problem. Try different things and if you can't go through it, think of a way to bypass the problem, work around it. You've got the tools now Ocean, just use the right ones for the right task. *Suerte.*'

'Thanks man,' he couldn't remember ever feeling this nervous before a test. What the hell would he do if he failed? *No. Be positive. You can do this.*

Warren stood at the front of the class. There was the empty space where Vasile had sat. Would Ocean's spot be the next to be vacated? The other students looked fairly calm. No wonder. They were all better than him at this stuff.

'Your test will last thirty minutes. You are about to face the same entrance exam that MI6 cyber-security candidates take, with a few tweaks courtesy of yours truly. Pass this third and final test and you can choose to formally join our program here. You'll have three problems to solve, and a decision to make. I'll say no more, other than good luck.' Warren sat at his desk. Either side of him, someone had stuck labels on the doors. The left was labelled *A*, the right *B*. Was this something to do with the test?

'Begin, n-ow.' Warren hit a key and each student's screen blinked to life. Dante was typing already but all Ocean saw was a screen full of gibberish.

The block of code was in binary format, some letters, some numbers and sometimes a mix of both. Underneath was an enterable field with **Keyword** next to it. So there was a keyword he needed to enter to unlock the code. Or maybe he had to decrypt the code and it would reveal a keyword he had to enter to move onto the next problem. He wasted a couple of minutes looking for visual patterns in the code, but it was useless. He scrolled down. The screen had a comments section with fifteen or so posts. That was odd. Why would they include that in the test? A distraction? Or perhaps, he thought more hopefully, it might provide a clue.

Some were inane and he could dismiss easily. 'Wow dude, that is tricky!' said one. A few comments had links attached to them. The first launched a browser window offering him Viagra tablets. The next link advertised a group of accident and injury lawyers. This was a waste of time ... but then he wasn't exactly spoilt for ideas. He tried the next link and up opened a webpage with encryption and decryption capability for the ARCFOUR decryption algorithm.

His heart lurched with excitement. He copied and pasted the code into the search field, hit decrypt and out spurted a single word. Orca.

Ocean typed 'Orca' into the keyword search and the code blew apart like a scared shoal of fish. One down, two to go. Eight minutes gone, that was good. He glanced over at Dante. His friend's eyes were wide, his hands off the keyboard and he was staring open-mouthed at the screen. Ocean tried to catch his eye, but Dante pushed back his chair, got to his feet and walked to the door labelled *B.* He'd finished already?

*Focus! Stop wasting valuable time.* Ocean wrestled his attention back to the screen. He diagnosed the second challenge instantly having gone over it with Dante the night before. There was a simple program with a fault but the source code was missing. That meant it was a reverse engineering task, retracing the binary code back to find the fault, to fix it and get the program running smoothly again. Knowing what to do was one thing, but doing it quickly against the clock quite another. The code was thankfully short but his corrections hadn't seemed to work. He ran a debugger, testing his new code line by line and found the culprit. An extra keystroke written in error and it had caused the whole thing to crash. Bloody code. It was like the old fashioned Christmas lights where one faulty bulb would knock out the whole line. The code fixed, the program ran and loaded up the final problem on the screen.

Claude got up, he too going through the door marked B. Then, as Ocean read his third challenge, Kaya followed too. Only he, Drew and Warren were left in the room. Ten minutes left. He took a deep breath. It was a mock-up of a login screen for a webpage. The words 'Hack me' were written at the top. A username was already filled in, but the password field was empty. It was down to this. Crack the password and he was in.

He opened up the source code for the page and scanned it for anything obvious, any security protocols he could over-ride. Nothing. Dante had shown him a password-breaking tool but it was a slow chugger; it took time to test billions of password combinations. Ten, no nine minutes wasn't going to be enough. Ocean tried the 'create a new account' link. If he could find out the password parameters then it would help to limit the search. A minimum of seven characters, one number and a maximum of twelve characters. *Good*, he thought excitedly. He loaded up the password software, inputted the new limitations and hit return. His heart dive-bombed. Estimated time to check: five days, four hours and twenty-one minutes. Out of the corner of his eye, Drew rose and he too, headed for door B.

Ocean checked his watch. Four minutes left. Come on! What else? What had Dante said? *If you can't go through it, think of a way to bypass the problem, work around it.* Work around it ... but how? Something popped into his head from one of Warren's classes, not something Dante had gone over with him ... something to do with buffering or something. He did a quick Google search. *Buffer Overflow.* That was it! The principle was simple; maybe that's why it had stuck in his mind. When some programs are written, they are given buffers for data to overflow into, like overflow channels for rivers. If he flooded these channels with data—breaking the banks—then it would overwrite the existing memory. He would flood that mother for all he was worth and hope to drift past the overwritten security protocols. He headed to *dark0de*—a hacker's sweet shop whose stockroom was pure dark web— and in seconds found a program that would do it for him. Ocean pasted the data in the password field and with a hammering heart, hit return. Nothing. The character limits on the password had protected it. He looked at his watch. One minute. Was there a limit on the username field too? In desperation, he deleted the username and pasted the data in there. Hit return. The screen went white.

'Come on, Come on,' he muttered.

Then, it refreshed with both username and password empty. Had it worked? The fields were empty. He hit return. And the screen went black. He held his breath. A message appeared.

Congratulations. You have completed the tasks and the clock has stopped. Do not look around. Do not let on yet that you have passed. You have an important decision to make.

It felt like a parade of ants were moving down his spine. Ocean didn't look around, though it hardly mattered as all the other students had finished.

The last two weeks you have been through a preliminary assessment for a special role in our organisation. Congratulations on passing this assessment. At this stage, you have the option to leave or to join us. Read on: then you will have five minutes to make your decision.

**Who are we?**

We are sensitive to your position: how do you join something when you are unsure what you are joining? Here we reveal the little we can to help you decide without compromising ourselves.

We are a team of extraordinary individuals with a single bold aim and are looking to grow our number. We bear no nationality, no flag and no political allegiances. You have been scouted, tested and are deemed suitable to join our noble cause, should you decide so. Our business must be kept secret here, though you may have an inclination based on the tests and classes you have taken so far.

**Join us?**

Your training salary will be £50,000 a year, plus bonuses. Your training will be of the highest quality. Expect travel. Your job and training must be a closely guarded secret from all but the organisation's operatives. The work is often dangerous. If you choose to join us, you will learn much but there can be no going back. Membership is a lifelong deal. The door to join us is door B.

**Or walk away?**

At this point, you can still walk away (through door A) by signing a binding Non-Disclosure Agreement about your time here and you'll receive a small payment for your discretion. To choose to walk away is as strong a decision as it is to stay. This life isn't for everyone.

There is much that is vague about this offer but some people commit to God with less thought or reasoning. Search within yourself for your instinctual answer. Five minutes may seem little to you to make a life altering decision. But any life can change in a second and often without the luxury of choice.

Choose wisely.

# 15

# NARNIA

Ocean read the message again. This felt like some sort of psychological riddle he didn't know the answer to: commit your life to something unknown to find out what it was or live parched with unquenched curiosity forevermore. The others had chosen easily enough and they didn't even have family bonds to contend with. Then why wasn't he sure? Hadn't he left home that summer to take a leap of faith, to find out who he might become? What else was there, if not this? He rose.

Warren watched him. Ocean stretched the skin around his Adam's apple, massaging it while his mind whirred. Two doors. One led to frustration, unanswered questions and security. The other led to knowledge, danger and the unknown. For some reason, his instinct was to walk away, to choose door *A*, but he couldn't say why. Stronger than instinct though, was the allure of the unknown. It pulled at him like a tidal current that he knew better than to swim against. He'd come this far hadn't he? He couldn't chicken out now.

Ocean took a breath at door *B*. It smelt of pine ... the metal handle was cold against his sweaty palm. In he went. He'd once supposed this space was full of servers, blinking light and wires. Sensor lights blinked on, illuminating concrete steps down to another metal door.

'Go on.' Warren urged. 'I'll be right behind you.'

With each step he questioned his choice but like an addict near a fix, he could not stop himself. At the bottom, he pressed his palm to a device on the wall. A light bibbed green, a lock retracted. They had his prints too.

This was it then. His own Narnian wardrobe. It opened without a sound.

What he saw seized his breath from his chest and held it there.

The basement was at least double the size of the farmhouse's ground floor. Stainless steel. Whitewashed walls. Spotlights. The hum of air conditioning. It felt like future.

A hand rested upon his shoulder. Warren. 'It's all brand new. Our new headquarters.'

Headquarters? He looked around for some clue. Sections with clear walls like he'd seen on squash courts. Behind one was a line of expressionless mannequins with target markings on their torsos. There were glass cabinets stacked with guns ranging from pistols to what looked like a telescopic sniper rifle. God … what had he done? What sort of noble cause needed so many guns? And then the next room was a lab of some kind. Bomb making? The thought barged into his head. Were they terrorists? Why hadn't he thought more carefully? What had the message said? Bold aims and noble causes? No allegiances, no nationalities, no flags?

'I'm not—' Ocean stepped back into Warren.

'You've made a choice you don't yet understand. You're a smart kid. Go ahead and join them for the briefing. See what you think then.'

Warren's voice was soothing, warm. He swallowed. Nodded. Answers. The floor was blindingly white and clean. A yellow, *Caution, Wet Floor!* sign stood astride a drain in the middle of the floor. Then he noticed Sue, the cook, at the far end of the room, mopping the floor. Her too? God this was surreal.

'Alright dearie?' she said.

His throat could find no useful sound so he just nodded, though he wasn't alright. He squeaked past a room with two banks of laptops facing a cinema style screen and then, finally, a conference room. Through the glass, Uncle Frank, Scarlet, Uri and the other students sat around a table. Dante beamed, his mouth moving.

'It's soundproofed.' Warren explained, behind him again like a shadow.

Ocean entered.

'Ha-ha! You did it!' said Claude.

'Take a seat,' Uncle Frank said, formally.

Ocean sunk into a leather office chair, the material creaking as it cushioned his weight.

'You left it late,' said Uri. 'We've already started the briefing.'

'Then you'll have to start it again,' Ocean's tone was cold and hard as a meteorite.

To his surprise, Uri smiled. 'Just like Jack,' with a nostalgic shake of his head. The pang he felt for his father hit him as suddenly as a slap. If only it were Jack Daley making sense of all this.

'I'm glad you're here Ocean,' Uncle Frank said. 'Welcome to Orca.'

## ORCA RISING

Orca. The keyword from the technical test. 'As in the killer whale?'

Uncle Frank assented with a nod. 'A good place to begin. Orca or killer whales are the most inspiring of species. A pod of Orca works together to find remarkable solutions to problems posed by their environment. Observe.' Uri killed the lights.

A video loaded up on a projector screen.

Icy sea. A jagged ice floe harboured a group of seals in its centre whilst a pod of orca circled around. In unison the orca bowed and dipped their noses into the sea, creating ripples and then as they synchronised their splashing, meatier waves slapped and sploshed against the ice floe. The platform see-sawed, the seals sliding one way, then the other, desperately seeking grip on the ice until all at once, it was too much. The seals slid one by one into the water with a plop. The dorsal fins dived and though beyond the reach of the camera, a feeding frenzy no doubt ensued.

The lights came back on. 'Ask any idiot off the street who the king predator of the sea is and they'll tell you it's the shark. But guess what?' Uncle Frank tapped his temple. 'Orca hunt great whites. Sharks only get oxygen when water is flowing over their gills. So what does our clever Orca do? It grabs the dumb shark by the tail, flips it upside down and holds it there for ten, fifteen minutes until it suffocates. Brutal, but ingenious. Orca roam the seas with grace and intelligence. That is why Jack and I admired them so, and chose to name our organisation Orca.'

So far, so David Attenborough. Ocean guessed this wasn't all a euphemism for seal clubbing though, where was it all leading? The other students in the room shifted in their seats.

'Who's Jack? That's the second time you've mentioned him,' asked Kaya.

'He was our co-founder, first leader and Ocean's father,' Scarlet said and Ocean felt all eyes in the room land on him. Of course. They didn't know. Something was new for him too, Dad had been the leader?

'Wait. So your father *and* uncle were in Orca? *Incroyable!*' said Claude. Ocean waited for a swipe from Drew but Uncle Frank headed it off.

'Orca needs new blood, the next generation to continue our work. That's why you're all here, Ocean is here on merit, not because of his family ties.'

'I actually only found out about it yesterday,' Ocean said apologetically, thinking that Dante might be hurt that he'd not said anything. 'But maybe we could get on with the whole, why are we here thing?'

Frank nodded. 'I have a simple and single-minded vision for our organisation and it's this,' he paused, steepling his hands on the desk. 'We want a future without war.'

A pause. Nobody laughed. Why was nobody laughing? Surely, this was absurd?

Ocean cleared his throat. 'How on earth can anyone hope to achieve that?'

'One bite at a time.' Uncle Frank had the calm air of somebody with total conviction in what he was saying and it had the curious effect of making Ocean take it more seriously too. And now that he did, he was suddenly relieved, like he'd been holding his breath too long and could finally come up for air. Achievable or not, at least the aim *was* a noble one. Orca was a force for good. His father had started it. Pride swelled in his chest.

'Our mainstay is surveillance services, hacking and espionage. We work on a case-by-case basis. If it furthers our aim of achieving a state of world peace then we do it. If not we don't.'

Ocean grinned from ear to ear, here was a life that would stretch him personally with the gargantuan benefit of doing something positive in the world. Destiny had intervened so he could pick up where his Dad had left off.

'It's an honour to welcome you to Orca,' Uncle Frank continued, 'and we're glad to have younger folk in our number now. You tend to draw less scrutiny than us oldies not to mention increasing our cultural reach. Can you imagine me spying on a mark at an indie concert, trying to crowd surf or whatever you kids do these days?'

They all laughed at that.

'But, you've been in soft-play until now. Things need to step up and accelerate.'

You don't say, Ocean thought. He'd seen the curriculum.

'Little by little, we'll turn you into professional spies. You'll lead double lives and undertake missions for Orca. You'll be paid handsomely, travel internationally, have your wits challenged on a daily basis and be a catalyst to world events.'

Excitement ebbed and flowed through his veins. *I'll be just like James Bond.*

'And this isn't any James Bond crap,' Uncle Frank went on. Could he read minds? 'This is for real. Don't expect tuxedoes, cocktails and screws in the shower. We move in silence and shadow. Our work is only done when nobody knows it is us who has done it.'

Awed silence.

'Frank?' Scarlet said after a few moments. 'A good time to share our words perhaps?'

Uncle Frank's mouth opened, revealing cigarette stained teeth. 'By shadow we craft a future of our own making.'

Scarlet, Uri and Warren covered their hearts with a hand and repeated: 'By shadow we craft a future of our own making.'

Introduction complete, Uncle Frank got up. 'Now that is all out in the open, your intensive training can begin in earnest tomorrow. Scarlet will explain how things will proceed. And Ocean?'

'Yeah?' he said it like he'd been drifting off in class; he hadn't expected to be singled out.

'We'll talk soon, I promise. You'll want to know about Jack.'

He nodded. 'Over a game of snooker perhaps.'

'That's the spirit,' he said and left.

Scarlet cleared her throat. 'Your schedules,' she handed out printouts of the timetable. Ocean and Dante exchanged a guilty glance and studied the paper as if it were the first time they had seen it.

'Scarlet?' Dante pointed at the line break. 'Field Missions?'

She looked to Uri and Warren, who both gave go-ahead shrugs.

'You can only learn so much in the classroom. Your first real-life assignment will take place before summer's end. Frank's accepting some easy, low-end jobs for you to cut your teeth. One of us will mentor you throughout. What do you guys think about that?'

## ORCA RISING

Ocean couldn't believe it! A mission before the end of the summer? Nervous energy swarmed within him. He placed his hand over his heart. The others did the same.

'By shadow we craft a future of our own making.'

# 16

# PRIDE

The schedule was loaded. On the first morning, the students implanted bugging devices into different smartphone models. Then in the afternoon they were learning the basics of Neuro-Linguistic Programming. There was a whole industry behind NLP designed to manipulate, influence and incept thoughts into others through the power of speech and gesture. Ocean didn't know if it was part hypnosis, part Jedi mind trick but a YouTube video of a famous illusionist doing it had him convinced. The illusionist managed to convince an actor he wanted a kid's red BMX bike for his birthday through his suggestive choice of words alone. This was no mumbo jumbo. It could actually work.

The mind taxed to its limit, the sessions with Uri then bludgeoned the body. The initial goal of the body combat classes was to give the diner a flavour of each ass-kicking technique from the world's martial arts buffet. Ocean, thinking he was pretty tough and would be good in a fight, learnt the opposite was true. He was roundhoused, punched, thrown, swept and barged to the mat with such inevitable regularity that he walked around in a permanence of bruises. Drew, already a wrestling expert, took particular pleasure in holding Ocean a second or two longer than was necessary in choke holds. Orca brethren they might now be, but Drew was still a complete tool.

It wasn't until the end of the week that Ocean got to speak to Uncle Frank alone.

'Rack 'em up.'

'You can break,' Ocean said.

Uncle Frank crouched over the cue. 'I'm glad we can talk freely now.' He struck the white cleanly; clipping the edge of the triangle of reds, back cushion, side cushion, top cushion and then coming to rest back in the D between the green and the yellow. Textbook.

'Me too.' Ocean chalked his cue with a twist of the hand, blew off the excess blue dust. He crouched, pulled back the cue and smacked the white down the table, clipped a tight red into the bottom pocket and eased back in line with the blue.

'You've been practicing.' Uncle Frank said in an accusatory tone.

'A couple of times,' he admitted. He'd been too bruised to run, so instead had played with Claude after class. The Frenchman didn't really get the tactical element of snooker. The safety play, the use of angles and covering seemed alien to him. For Claude it was just about potting and the more outlandish the better, regardless of where the white ended up. Though the games weren't close, Ocean used it as practice to give Uncle Frank a better game the next time they met over the green baize.

'That's five minutes without you asking the question burning a hole in your throat.'

'I figured you'd start when you're ready to talk. Pressing you doesn't get me anywhere.'

106

Uncle Frank tipped up his hat and scratched under the brim line. 'You're getting to know me Ocean. Knowledge of someone is your personal map to their hopes, comforts and fears, their soul even. It's how you get what you want from people. Jack was great at that too.'

'I'm learning. Slowly.' Ocean dispatched the blue and leant on the cue. 'But Dad... Jack. I...' he didn't know what he wanted to say.

Frank rested a hand on his shoulder. 'I know exactly how you feel.'

'He's always there at the back of my mind, you know? I feel like I might just be able to reach him and pull him closer somehow. But he's always beyond my fingertips or not there at all. I was thinking that maybe it was because I didn't know how he really died. But maybe that's not it at all. Maybe it's because I don't know how he really lived.'

Uncle Frank frowned. 'Wise thoughts for a young head. Are you saying you don't want to know how he died?'

'No,' Ocean braced himself. 'I want to know the truth.

'You're sure?'

'I'm ready.'

'It happened in Bolivia,' Uncle Frank shook his head. 'We must have done eighty or ninety missions together, Jack and me. I was on tactical in a downtown loft in La Paz, he was on point.'

Bolivia. Uncle Frank's stretch in prison was there. He did the maths; it had to have been at the same time.

'The job involved us taking out a corrupt politician.'

'Taking out?'

'Just planting some evidence, tip off some journos that he was in with the cartels. Get him sent to jail or at least fired from his job in the public domain. Something he couldn't wheedle out of with bribes.'

Wow. Was this the kind of thing he'd have to do? How did it relate to stopping war? It wasn't the time for such questions.

'So we're mid-op, Jack's in the official's house doing the plant.' Uncle Frank leant on his snooker cue as if needing its strength. 'All of a sudden he tells me he's got company. I hear him breathing. I can tell he's scared. I hear muffled movement. Then gunfire. Three shots. Pop, pop, pop.'

And there it was. The freight train of grief. Three years late. Ocean clenched his fists at his sides, bit down, too angry to cry.

'I say his name,' Uncle Frank went on, his voice now hoarse. 'I shout it, "Jack! Come in, Jack" and then they kicked in my door.'

Ocean squeezed the cue tight enough to splinter. 'Who?'

'Three Bolivian guys in green army fatigues, all pointing assault rifles at me. They arrested me and the rest, you know. I spent a few years in that crap hole of a prison.'

Silence hung heavy as fog. Could he ask it? He could. 'This will sound mean but why shoot Dad and not you?'

'He had a gun. I had a computer. Look, I don't know what happened in that room for sure. All I know is they got him. I identified the body. Two bullet wounds, here and here.' Uncle Frank indicated his chest and just above the hip.

Was Uncle Frank telling him everything? 'But how did the army guys know where you were?'

Uncle Frank shook his head. 'We were betrayed, Christ knows how. It was all I thought about in prison for the first year or so, but I couldn't figure it out. I had to let it go in the end or it would've consumed me. I'd have never gotten out of that place, never restarted Orca and continued Jack's work.'

Ocean nodded. Frank had moved on. But how? Surely you couldn't if someone had killed your own brother? But he couldn't find the heart to say it. After all, he was a teenager, what did he know of the conditions in a Bolivian prison? Perhaps it was all Uncle Frank could do to survive and he could hardly begrudge him that.

'How did you get out?'

'Nothing glamorous. A few well-placed bribes. A good lawyer. A softening of the Morales regime towards me after a few years.'

The snooker balls seemed to have lost their sheen somehow. His poor dad. Buried somewhere in Bolivia.

'You see. An IED in Afghanistan was a nicer thing to believe, horrible though it was to have to do that to you and your Mam.'

Mum. He hadn't called in days, he realised. Later. He'd do it later. 'Why does she hate you so much?'

'One for Scarlet I think. Transference of guilt? Projection? She couldn't blame or hate Jack so she took it out on me instead.'

'That's stupid.'

'Skye's a lovely girl, but you and I both know she's not the most logical of thinkers.'

Picking Andy as your life partner was not evidence of a sharp and logical mind. He missed her all of a sudden. 'I wonder what she'll say when I tell her I'm not doing my A-Levels. She'll probably go ballistic.'

Uncle Frank shook his head. 'No need. You'll do your A-Levels.'

'But what about training?'

'Oh you'll be trained, don't worry about that. You lead a double life now Ocean. You're not someone people are going to wonder about. You are going to be Ocean Daley, a normal teenage kid who happens to have some skills on the side that he gets paid very handsomely for. Going to school, being who you already are is the cover you'll need to cultivate.'

Ocean deflated further. He had to go back to school too? He was so far beyond its reach now.

'It'll keep peoples' guard down around you, everyone underestimates a school kid. It'll keep your Mam happy and it won't be a waste of time. What were you thinking of studying?'

Ocean sighed. 'If I *had* to stay I would have done History, English and Geography.'

Uncle Frank shook his head. 'No. You'll need to do something more useful. Languages, Chemistry, Biology. How many can you do?'

'Four I think, most people do three.'

'Do five.'

Ocean was taken aback. 'Five?'

'You're doing them for yourself, for me, for this job, not for that stupid school. If you want to be trained, that's what I need you to do.'

'But how will I have time to train if I'm juggling five A-Levels?'

'By being exceptional. Commitment is the cost of greatness. You'll have to be dedicated, because we'll ask a lot of you. We'll do remote learning some evenings, we do a lot of theory. The occasional weekend I'm sure we can smuggle you up here. During school holiday's we will do intensives, and missions, well, they happen when they need to happen.'

In Ocean's head it was going to be A-Levels *or* spy training. A normal life *or* a secret one. A life in Shoreham *or* a life of jet-setting intrigue. He was quickly learning that things weren't binary with Uncle Frank, there was no *either/or*, there was just *and*. If he did this, he would have to do and be everything he possibly could. And, a thought lurked. If he got good enough, perhaps he could find out what really happened in Bolivia and who was behind his father's death.

'I'd be proud to.'

Uncle Frank bear hugged him. 'That's the spirit! You can't know how good it is to have you here. My protégée. Our future! Jack's legacy. I predict special things.'

'I hope so,' Ocean resumed play.

'You know something?'

Ocean looked up from the cue. 'What?'

'Your dad would have been so proud of you.'

They had Saturday morning off. It was a glorious day but Ocean felt sombre, as bruised on the outside as in. Though he was still too sore to run, walking was a decent lo-fi substitute. He was getting stronger and the combat contests getting a little closer. His body was toughening up to the beating. Just like Rocky. Sly's voice echoed in his head: *It ain't about how hard you hit: it's about how hard you can get hit and keep moving forward!* Well, he'd taken a Rocky style pounding and he was still moving forward. Just about.

The grass had lost its lustre, now dry and wine-coloured from the good summer weather. A herd of deer started at the sound of his footsteps and drained into a copse. His phone buzzed in his pocket. Mum. He had meant to call her.

'Hiya,' he winced, waiting for an earful.

'O, honey, can you talk?' She sounded breathy.

111

'Sure,' he relaxed a little, 'what's up?'

'Well, there's a letter here for you.' Pause. 'I think it might be your exam results.'

He had totally forgotten about his exams, so much had happened since then. 'Right, I see.'

'I know some people can be a bit superstitious about opening them, so it can wait until you get home if you like or I can open it for you, tell you the results over the phone or I could email a photo of them or something.' She was babbling.

'You've opened them already haven't you?'

'Oh O! I'm sorry I couldn't help it. It was there all morning just tempting me, then Caroline from the club called and you know her son Steven was getting his results today too and she was boasting down the phone and asking how you'd got on and Andy told me not to, but as soon as he went out, I just—'

'Mum! Just tell me! How did I do? Were they alright?'

'Oh Ocean!' she said again, she couldn't hold it together, she was blubbing, 'bewwthenawwight!'

'What? I can't understand you! Just tell me they were alright, would you?'

Two sharp intakes of breath. Whimpering. Then: 'Better. Than. Alright.' Her voice was fragile as glass, like it might break any second.

He smiled. 'Are you enjoying this? Such a drama-queen, this isn't the X Factor. Come on, spill.'

Each word came out with a staccato breath: 'Five—A— stars,' another sob, 'and—six—A's!' Then she was off again, crying uncontrollably down the phone.

Ocean found he was beaming with joy, he knew the exams had gone well enough but he'd never expected grades as high as that.

'Get in!'

She blew her nose. '*The Shoreham Herald* and *The Argus* wanted to interview you, shame you're not here. Oh honey, I am so sorry I opened them. You are just such a clever little currant I knew you'd have done well!'

'Mum, seriously, it's fine. You know I don't mind about that sort of thing. And listen,' he knew she would want to hear this, 'I decided yesterday, even before the results, that I'm going to stay on and do my A-Levels.'

She was off again. He rolled his eyes, waited for her to return. And then, when she was back.

'Your dad would have been so proud of you.'

# 17

# MIKE MYSTERY

The following week was as intense as the last, but come Thursday, something strange happened. The students were lined up, shooting blank tranquiliser darts at the mannequins, when Warren interrupted the class.

'Ocean. Dante. Join me in the conference room.'

Ocean exchanged a look with his friend that communicated it all: we've been busted. How serious a punishment would they cop for hacking into the computer system before the test? Expulsion?

Scarlet was waiting for them.

'Morning gentlemen.'

'Morning Scarlet.'

Dante was calm. Ocean remembered he'd beaten the lie detector twice. Smart. Keep quiet. See what they know first.

'We're pulling you both from your current schedule of classes.'

Ocean panicked. 'What?'

'Why?' asked Dante.

'The first mission has come in on the wire.'

Ocean took a second to rearrange his face. He wasn't going to be expelled! Then, a mission? The worry of it all melted away, leaving just the bare rock of excitement.

'It's going to be a joint mission.' Warren said. 'You two worked well together in passing the tests. You'll make a good team.'

'Like Dad and Uncle Frank.' Ocean said.

'Better than that I hope. They only did a few missions together. Jack mostly worked with Uri and me,' Warren said.

Ocean was confused, hadn't Uncle Frank said eighty or ninety? Or had he said eight or nine and Ocean had just misheard?

Warren went on: 'For your mission we need to accelerate your learning in certain specialisms. Dante, you'll have two days with me in the computer lab, I need to test you on some pretty specific skills.'

'And you Ocean, will be with me,' said Scarlet.

'Specific skills I need to learn too?'

'Yes. I'll be the mentor for you both on the mission. But Dante with his superior computer skills will be on tactical. You'll be on point.'

At the sharp end of the action. Just like Dad.

Ocean's first private lesson wasn't in the basement, but up in the farmhouse lounge. Waiting for him was a man in a scruffy white shirt and black waistcoat combination. He wore eyeliner and stuffed his messy jet-black hair under a burgundy beret.

'Ocean. This is Mike Mystery,' Scarlet said, 'well, that's his stage name. He's a professional magician. He's going to train you to be competent at sleight of hand.'

'What's that?' Ocean asked.

Mike Mystery held out a hand, ignoring his question. 'Pleased to make your acquaintance Ocean.'

Ocean shook it and in the same instant Mike Mystery pulled a rubber duck out from Ocean's own sleeve.

'What! How did you do that?' Ocean laughed, checking Mike's sleeves, but they were pulled up beyond the forearm.

Mike smiled and cocked an eyebrow. 'Like that did you? The toddlers love it at birthday parties.' He gazed at the yellow rubber duck, dusted his hands together and the duck disappeared again. Impossible. He'd been watching Mike's every move.

'That my young friend is sleight of hand. Are you ready to get started?'

It was a frustrating thing to learn. His hands weren't quick enough. There was a whole anatomical universe of hand muscles he never knew existed. They ached constantly as he grappled with the different grips and finger movements involved in making an object disappear in front of the naked eye. Mike Mystery repeated his motto: 'Practice, practice, practice,' a million times that morning. Ocean *was* practicing. It was all he was doing. Even for a fast learner like himself, a morning's practice would never accomplish the same results as years of training. But little by little, he grasped the basics and by lunchtime he could just about make a credit card disappear by only rubbing one palm over the other.

'Good. Very good indeed,' declared Mike, 'there is plenty you must still work on, so—'

'Practice, practice, practice I know.'

Ocean took the annoying advice to heart, trying his new moves under the lunch table with a spoon. It didn't go unnoticed.

'You fiddling with yourself again Ocean? How many times have I got to tell you? Not at the dinner table.' Drew was pleased with himself for that one.

Ocean let him have that round. He looked forward to the day when it'd be his knee pressing down on Drew's windpipe.

The afternoon session with Mike Mystery graduated from sleight of hand to what Ocean could only describe as pick pocketing. Apparently, Mike Mystery hadn't always been a magician.

Mike broke the procedure down to four stages. 'First is the observation. What are you liberating? If it's a wristwatch, on what arm is it? What type of clasp? If it's a pen or a wallet or a phone, when does the target take the item out? Which pocket is it kept in?'

This was the kind of stuff he'd learnt to notice in Scarlet's classes anyway.

'Second is the plan. When is the best moment to make your move? Where are your escape routes if you get made? How will you do it? Do you need to switch the item for a replica? Will you need a distraction?'

Ocean remembered losing his MP3 player once, it was on his table at lunch wrapped up in his headphones. Then some year eight boy had tripped, launching his lunch tray into the air, the cutlery, plates and drink exploded onto the tiles. Naturally, everyone took the mick, a loud 'Waaaah!' resounded around the canteen. And then, when Ocean turned back, his music player was gone. Maybe, he now thought, that year eight kid had done it on purpose in league with a friend? Or maybe it was just an opportunist.

'Third is the execution. We will spend most of our time this afternoon on this aspect. We'll have time to cover the body bump, the distraction, the solo pick and the double pick. You'll use some of the skills you learnt this morning.'

'And the fourth element?'

'Getting away cleanly. The escape, if you like. Let's get to work.'

The pattern was a similar one. To start off with Ocean was clumsy and heavy-handed. Mike placed a wallet in different pockets of his jacket or trousers and would close his eyes while Ocean tried to affect a pick of said wallet without setting off Mike's internal alarms. He would get it out the pocket, but Mike would feel it. He would try dropping a counterweight into the pocket the same time as he pulled the wallet out, only to drop the bugger on the floor with a splat. He was the actor who couldn't quite get his lines right at rehearsals in front of a finicky director.

'Again,' Mike would say.

'Too heavy-handed.'

'Too slow.'

'Too fast.'

'You're joking aren't you? That was the worst one yet.'

'Felt that.'

'Too noisy.'

'Nearly. Try again.'

'Smoother. Slide the wallet out. Don't tug it or it'll jam on the fabric.'

'No. Again.'

Until finally, at half past three. 'Did you just do it?' Mike opened an eye. 'I didn't feel a thing.'

Ocean threw the wallet up and down in his hand like a tennis ball. 'Your wallet has been liberated from Guantánamo pocket.'

'At the risk of making you cocky, it normally takes someone a week to do that.'

He grinned.

'Wipe that off your face and do it again. Prove to me it wasn't a fluke.'

And so he did.

After dinner, he and Dante snuck down into the basement and into the soundproofed conference room. Ocean told him all he'd been learning that day and his certainty that his end of the mission was to steal something off someone.

'And you?'

'I spent all day hacking individual mobile phones. Listening into conversations, reading text messages, disabling them and controlling them remotely. It was actually pretty easy. I could do some stuff that even Warren didn't know how to do.'

'I wonder what they'll want us to do.'

'I could do a little digging? I think I could get past most of Warren's security protocols.'

Ocean shook his head, they'd gotten lucky once hacking into the Orca computers but it didn't guarantee they'd be successful again. 'They'll probably tell us tomorrow anyway. Let's just wait.'

The following morning, Ocean found his workstation set up with an iPhone, a mini screwdriver and a rectangular surveillance device he'd never seen before, larger and flatter than usual. Scarlet gestured him to sit and begin. Ocean removed the mini screws and prised open the device with tweezers. He levered up the battery, noticing it was the exact same size as the bug. Scarlet gave him a nod, and Ocean slipped the device underneath. He laid the battery down over the bug and clipped the case shut, replaced the screws and the job was done.

'Twenty-two seconds,' Scarlet observed.

He hadn't realised he was being timed. 'Is that good?'

'You need to do it in less than ten. Practice all morning until you can.'

'Practice, practice, practice,' Ocean sighed.

It took him half the morning to break the ten second mark. He did it three more times just to make sure he'd got it and sought out Scarlet.

'Good. I'll get the others. Meet us in the conference room. It's time for your briefing on the mission.'

# 18

# MISSION BRIEF

The projector hummed. Dust swirled in the beam. Light scattered onto a screen, forming a face.

'Meet your mark,' Warren said.

Ocean narrowed his eyes. It was a black and white shot taken with a telescopic lens as the man walked out of a revolving door. The mark had a sleazy look to him; pinstripe suit, stubble shadow and greasy hair held in place by sunglasses.

'Meet one Kenneth Slater. He's a journalist. Works for one of the red tops,' said Scarlet.

'Red tops?' asked Dante.

'Tabloid newspapers. Kenny here has been a naughty boy. His normal trick is celeb and sports star exposés, but he's branching out. Slater's hacked the voicemail of a politician and heard something he shouldn't.'

'So the politician is the client?' Ocean asked.

Scarlet nodded. 'His name's confidential but let's call him Joe. He's someone who has proved to be sympathetic to our cause in the past and we want to help.'

Ocean rubbed his chin. What had this politician done, voted against the Iraq invasion perhaps?

'So here's the background,' Scarlet continued, 'Joe is a married man with a pregnant wife. He's also gay. Not even his wife knows. If it gets out, it'll be a huge scandal and sink our asset.'

'So the voicemail ...' Ocean didn't need to finish his thought.

'Yep,' Warren took over, 'our hack Kenny hit the mother lode when he broke into Joe's voicemail. He picked up a message from Joe's lover.'

'Careless on Joe's part, but we are where we are. But here's the interesting thing boys, Slater hasn't gone to press yet.'

'Why not?' asked Dante.

'We've got a few theories,' Scarlet replied. 'We think he's waiting until just before the elections. The risk of getting scooped is small and the impact will be magnified tenfold.'

Uncle Frank had said these would be "low-end" jobs to start with but Ocean was surprised that this was spy agency material. They must really owe this politician big.

'So I'm guessing from my lessons that I need to bug his phone?'

'Just so. Our client, Joe, is in the dark about Slater's intentions. Bugging his phone gives us intel into what he's planning. Once Joe knows, he can plan for it. He could even come out to the press and his wife first and take control of the narrative. Information is power here.'

'Who knows,' Warren added, 'maybe we'll kick some dirt up on Slater that we can bargain with on the client's behalf.'

'Why do we need to bug the phone? Is there not something we can do remotely?' asked Dante.

Warren pulled a face. 'We've tried. Slater's no fool. He routes his calls through a private network service. We need to physically have the handset to bypass it. That's why we need Ocean.'

'So once I've planted the bug you guys can just do the do?'

'That's about the sum of it.'

'So where do we do this?'

Scarlet was about to say, but instead clicked onto the next slide. Blueprints appeared on the screen: a circle and an oblong with walkways in between. A stadium, or more accurately stadia. Oddly familiar too. He bent his head to one side and realised with a rush of adrenaline where it was.

'Bloody hell,' he said. 'Centre Court and Court One. That's Wimbledon.'

Things sprang into action fast. Uncle Frank drove Ocean, Dante and Scarlet to the train station in the Mustang. At the drop off area, Uncle Frank got out the car and gave Scarlet a kiss on the lips—something that Ocean watched in nothing short of wide-eyed amazement. Those two? Really?

'What you staring at?' Uncle Frank growled.

'Er ... nothing, I didn't realise that you two were uh ...'

Scarlet smiled and picked up her bag. 'I'll get the tickets boys. And you, I'll see in a few days,' she squeezed Uncle Frank's hand and headed to the ticket machines.

'Dante, would you give me a minute alone with Ocean?'

'Sure.' Dante threw his bag over his shoulder and took off.

Uncle Frank shades slid down his nose so his electric blue eyes shone over the rims. An X-ray would have been less penetrating.

'Ocean. Things are about to get real very fast. But I know you can do it. I see it in you. You have it, by God you have it, just like your dad. All that talent. It's in the blood.'

Was it? Haemoglobin was in the blood. White and red blood cells were in the blood. But talent? 'If you say so.'

'I do say so. Listen to Scarlet.'

'I will.'

Uncle Frank grabbed the back of Ocean's head and whispered in his ear. 'By shadow we craft a future of our own making.'

Frank slid back in the Mustang and gunned the engine. 'Make us proud,'

Us? He meant Jack too, Ocean realised. 'I will.'

Uncle Frank leaned out the window. 'I'll be watching.' The Mustang roared out of Leicester station in a trail of blue smoke.

The carriage rocked. So this was it then. He was a spy now and on his first real mission. He was desperate to talk about it, but of course he couldn't. He remembered studying posters for a project on the Second World War at school. *Loose Lips Sink Ships*. If there were such a thing as a job spec for a spy, he imagined the ability to keep shtum was pretty fundamental.

Would he have a code name? What if it was something awful? He imagined himself in Vienna or St. Petersburg, sitting in the corner of a dingy bar and a contact coming in, wearing a Macintosh and a hat, taking the next booth to him and mumbling: 'Are you the man they've sent us?' and him having to reply, 'Yes. It's me. I'm …. [he sighs] … I'm NightHawk.'

What had gotten into him, these stupid thoughts whizzing haphazardly through his mind? The English countryside blurred past. A pasture, a new housing development, golden fields of oil seed rape and a muddy lake. Dante was asleep with headphones in. Scarlet's nose was in a book. Ocean picked up a free paper another passenger had left and flipped it, starting with the sports at the back. There were articles about Wimbledon, charting Harper's progress through the draw. **Will it be Harper's year?** Ocean couldn't be bothered to read it. The next article read: **Wimbledon Chief asked to stand down**. It covered how the chairman of the All England Club, Lord Cloudsley, who also held a role as a Labour peer, was being asked to stand down from his role at Wimbledon over doubts about his ability to fulfil the roles of both obligations. Apparently Cloudsley always took two weeks off from his political responsibilities to oversee the Wimbledon operation. This year however, Cloudsley was a key opponent to some bill or other that was coming through the House of ... blah, blah, blah. He moved on to the Silverstone Grand Prix and ditched the paper, turned up his music and let the miles tick by.

At Kings Cross, Scarlet took the first taxi. Ocean and Dante waited ten minutes and took another. At Holborn, Ocean paid the black cab in cash and hoisted his canvas bag on his shoulder. People flocked in and out of lunchtime eateries and coffee houses, dashed in front of red buses, beeping traffic and to the tube. Yep, this was London alright.

'Is that it over there?' Dante pointed.

Ocean checked the map on his phone. It was. The entrance to the safe house was between two shops. Ocean pressed the penthouse call button and they both crowded together to stare dumbly into the camera. The door buzzed and they pushed in, racing each other to the lift.

The safe house wasn't an attention grabber: two small bedrooms, a shared bathroom and a smog-smeared window overlooking the busy Holborn road.

'Catch,' Scarlet tossed a set of keys to them each. 'Don't lose them.'

Ocean and Dante dumped their things in the twin room. When they came back Scarlet was staring into the fridge. 'Good,' she declared, clipping it shut. 'They've stocked us enough for the basics, but we can't waste time cooking. We'll have to order in. Any preference?'

'Vietnamese or Thai? I'm not overly fussy though.'

Dante shrugged. 'Whatever, nothing too spicy.'

Scarlet nodded to a tablet on the kitchen worktop. 'One of you order for us and can the other pop over the road and get me a latte? It'll probably be a late night, there's a lot to cover.'

'A latte night huh?' Dante said with a grin.

'Dude.' Ocean shook his head with disdain. 'For that, you get to be the coffee boy.'

'You know how hard it is to make a pun in a foreign language?' Dante sighed but accepted his fate. Ocean ordered a Penang Curry, a Pad Thai for Dante, Chilli Aubergines and Thai Fish Cakes from an online menu. There was already a payment account set up, the address saved. Even spies had to eat.

Scarlet wheeled out a table loaded with high-tech equipment: flatscreens, laptops, headsets and a router.

'Nice set up.'

'Dante will run tactical from here, we've got a private fibre cable so the connection is secure.'

'Where will you be?'

'Here too, overseeing things. I'm like a driving instructor. Here to guide and suggest, but in the passenger seat. I have the emergency pedals should I need to step in—which I very much doubt—Dante seems to be something of a prodigy from what Warren tells me. I might even learn a thing or two myself.'

'Yeah, he's pretty amazing.'

'You guys are going to start giving me a big head.' Dante stood at the door and held up a cardboard tray with three cups wedged in. 'Espresso delivery!'

Ocean looked at Scarlet, the ghost of a grin was on her face. 'I hope he won't be making awful jokes the whole mission.' She plucked a cup from the tray, took a quick sip and gasped like she'd been in the desert and just found water. 'God that's worth the burn. Let's get down to business shall we?'

They all took a seat in the lounge with their coffees.

'So, here's what we know. Slater's definitely going to be at the men's final—that's two days away. There are two press areas. One for post-match conferences on the ground floor, the other is on the second floor in press hospitality. Ocean, Warren and I believe that getting you in as an employee is our best play. Real pass, real reason to be around the general press areas. We've reviewed the potential jobs and found the perfect thing, exactly the sort of behind-the-scenes job a teenager would do at Wimbledon.'

'Great, what is it?'

'Hold your horses. There's a catch. The tournament is almost over, there's already someone doing the job right now. You're just the backup in case he calls in sick.'

'Sounds like we need to encourage somebody to have a sick day,' said Dante.

'Just so. And I can tell you exactly who.'

That evening, Ocean loitered outside Gate 7 on Church Road, SW19. A few people still leaked out of Wimbledon Tennis Club.

127

Drunken old boys in matching blue blazers and chinos, a group of young shift workers, perhaps from one of the bars, even two young kids out past their bedtime with their parents, the boy cradling a gigantic tennis ball with a signature scrawled over the yellow fuzz.

Then a lad drifted out, a face Ocean, Scarlet and Dante had studied on the guy's Facebook account earlier that day in the Holborn flat. His name was Matty Adams, a year older than Ocean but somehow younger-looking in his ill-fitting suit and lanky limbs, like different parts of his body had growth spurted at different times. Matty walked with a stoop, tired maybe from his day at work. Headphones in, eyes trained a foot or two ahead of his dragging feet. Ocean's first mark. The person blocking him from a job at Wimbledon.

Instead of following Matty, Ocean walked in front of him. After all, he knew exactly where Matty was headed. It had been staggeringly easy. Matty's mobile number was openly listed on his Facebook page and it took Dante all of ten minutes to have the guy's texts and Whatsapp messages in front of them. From the hacked messages, a simple plan had emerged from an exchange between Matty and his Mum.

*Mum: Shall I leave u some dinner?*

*Matty: No thnx, I'll go to Chicken Hse on way 2 tube. X*

There was only one branch of *Chicken House* on the way to the tube station. Its white and blue sign with a red crowned cockerel was so bright, Ocean could see it a mile off. A glance back. Matty was still there, blissfully oblivious. Ocean pushed through the greasy metal doors. Salty warmth and frying fat. If he wasn't so nervous it might have made him hungry. A few customers were perched on stools, tearing into chicken or dangling chips into their mouths.

'Yes boss?'

Ocean squinted up at the menu. Showtime. 'Yes mate. Two piece meal combo with Sprite please.'

'£2.89 boss.'

Ocean paid cash, scooped the change. The server tonged two fried chicken legs from a metal cabinet and dropped them into a paper box. Chips and a drink appeared on a tray with his box of chicken. He tried a chip, piping hot, and pulled a face.

'Needs more salt that.'

Behind him, road traffic noise peaked then faded again with the clip of the door shutting. Matty Adams was in the building.

The server nodded over to a saltshaker.

'Add yourself boss.'

This was the tricky part. He reached over to the shaker but from his sleeve pulled out an identical one. Practice, practice, practice! Damn Mike Mystery, but he was glad for it now. He covered the chips generously with the crystalline chemical and salt mixture Scarlet had concocted for him and sleight of handed the shaker back into his jacket.

Someone stepped behind him. Tinny music seeped from headphones. Matty. Right on time. He hadn't counted on Matty listening to music, which weakened the next part of his plan. There was nothing he could do but play it through anyway.

'Actually mate, I don't want these chips.' Ocean said to the server.

'But you already pay.'

'Yeah, but I only wanted the chicken and the drink.'

The server looked confused. 'Chip included in meal deal. Same price with chip or no chip.'

Ocean sighed. 'Fine then I guess.' He turned to face Matty whose glazed eyes were anchored on the menu.

'Hey.'

Matty's expression was set to: *are you talking to me?*

Ocean nodded, made good eye contact and smiled. Matty removed his earphones.

'Yeah?'

'I just got these chips by mistake. I don't want them.' Ocean pointed to his untouched tray. 'I've already paid but the guy won't take them back, so if you want them you can have them for free. Otherwise they'll just go in the bin.'

Matty computed this. 'Oh no, that's alright thanks, I'm buying some of my own anyway.'

Ocean swallowed his panic; there was enough doubt in Matty's voice to suggest he was only being polite. Ocean kept his expression bland like it made no difference to him either way. 'Okay, I'll just bin them then.' He gave a half-turn. 'You sure? Last chance.'

Matty shifted on his feet. 'You're really going to chuck them?'

'Definitely. I just come for the chicken.'

A pause. *Come on Matty, you know you want them.*

Matty scratched the back of his neck. 'Well, no point them going to waste. Thanks man. Saves me buying them I guess.'

Ocean slid the chips from his tray onto next. 'No worries. Enjoy.'

Supressing excitement, Ocean took a spot by the window. It had worked. This was exactly what Scarlet covered in her classes: influencing others through your tone and NVC to get what you wanted. He was a beginner for sure, but he'd planned it and Matty had played right to his script!

Ocean tore into the first of his chicken legs, Henry VIII style. In the reflection of the window he watched Matty Adams take his tray to a table.

*Come on now Matty, eat your chips like a good boy.*

Matty popped a chip in his mouth, nodded with obvious satisfaction and then took another.

It was as easy as that.

# 19

# FIELD RECON

Ocean got up a little before six to get showered and dressed. A charcoal grey suit and two white shirts hung ready in his cupboard, the sizes right on the money. From *M & S*, he noticed. A small touch, but exactly the sort of parent-bought uniform a teenager might wear. Orca thought deep. Prepped safe houses, took telescopic photographs of marks and arranged jobs at short notice ... he felt like he was just seeing the head of an octopus and the tentacles moved unseen, arranging things in the inky underwater.

He couldn't wait for the proper mission. Slater sounded like a nasty piece of work. And wasn't there also some kind of poetic justice in taking down a phone hacker by hacking them back? Matty Adams was an unlucky extra in the film, haplessly caught in the crossfire of something much bigger than he realised. But he'd recover in a week or so. Ocean couldn't help but think of the film *Fight Club* where Brad Pitt's character, Tyler Durden was fond of saying: 'You wanna make an omelette, you gotta break some eggs!' There was some truth in that. Some collateral damage was inevitable, but as long as nobody got seriously hurt, it was fine by him.

Once dressed, Ocean joined Scarlet and Dante in the lounge where they could all stare at his phone on the coffee table and will it to ring with three sets of eyes.

'Remember, today is as much about familiarisation with the place as it is recon. Get used to the equipment, scope out the press areas and learn your duties.'

Ocean nodded, he wiped his palms on his trousers. Why wouldn't the bloody phone ring? He checked his watch. Two minutes past seven. Had Matty not called in sick yet? Had the saltshaker concoction not had the desired effect?

'Dante will be on tactical but I'll be listening in.'

'I got your back *tío*.'

'Thanks guys.'

The phone blinked into life. His heart leapt, he looked at them both.

'Answer it.'

Ocean hit the green symbol.

'Yes?'

'That's right.'

'I'm sorry to hear about that, but yes, I am available.'

'Sure, I'd be happy to fill in.'

'Of course. I can be there by eight, maybe quarter-past depending on the tube.'

'Great. The reception at Centre Court. Got it. I'll see you there Andrea, thanks.'

He hung up and puffed out his cheeks. 'We're on.'

As a rule Ocean didn't drink coffee, he loved the smell and its bitter bite but he'd read somewhere that whilst it made your energy levels peak, it also made them crash too. Perhaps it was the remnants of adrenaline from pulling off his mini-mission with Matty, or maybe it was the excitement of what would come next, but he hadn't slept much. Coupled with the early start he decided to buy a bucket of the stuff from a *Costa* by the tube. Dante joined him in the line to get Scarlet her latte.

'Keep your eyes open *tío*. Sound the situation out.'

'You think?' Ocean replied sarcastically.

'I mean from our point of view. Not Orca's.'

'Our point of view? But we are Orca?'

Dante wrung his fingers. 'I don't know *tío*. I just got to wondering, they were too quick to dismiss a remote hack of Slater's phone, with time I could have maybe figured something out. And why Wimbledon? Surely there are a hundred better times and places to do this sort of thing?'

'What's gotten into you? Chill out, it's just nerves. Orca are pros, we just need to stay confident and do what they tell us.'

'You're probably right.'

But Dante still looked concerned. Maybe he didn't have the guts for all this. Perhaps helping his friend to pass initiation was a mistake, the Spaniard's ability had been artificially raised by Ocean's help ... but then wasn't that also true of himself? He wouldn't have passed without Dante's help either.

'Try not to worry,' he rested a hand on Dante's shoulder. 'I've got this.'

The Central Line train rumbled west. The tube was mercifully cool with enough room to stand comfortably. Half the people piled off at Oxford Circus and Ocean grabbed a seat for the last few stops to Notting Hill Gate. Here he changed and took the District Line train to Wimbledon, already brimming with people heading to the tennis. Cool bags. Peach chinos. Straw hats. Sunglasses clipped to shirt pockets. A bag with sun lotion and a copy of *The Times* popping out. There was a feeling of happy expectation, some ambient pollen of good-humoured Britishness that Ocean might have enjoyed under different circumstances.

'Are you going to the tennis dear?' The lady was in a yellow dress, late sixties, he guessed.

'Sort of. I'm working there.'

'Oh yes? In the bar or one of the restaurants is it?'

'Something like that.'

'But they do let you watch some of the matches I hope?'

'You can catch a bit on the big screen from Henman Hill if you're on a long enough break,' he improvised.

'Oh no, it's not Henman Hill anymore. Or Murray Mount! It's Harper's Hill! How do you think he'll do in tomorrow's final?'

'Harper's probably not ready just yet. Maybe next year.'

It was like she'd been slapped, but luckily, the train had arrived.

'Well enjoy,' Ocean said, stepping out with the crowd.

It was a fair walk to the gate. An email confirmation on his phone got him his staff pass and he entered the complex. It was strangely quiet, too early to let the horde in. A few *G4S* security staff wandered about looking as if they'd been plucked randomly from the street and squeezed into badly made uniforms. A small crew from the BBC filmed Sue Barker talking animatedly into the camera. No time for that. He made a beeline for Centre Court. He had a job to do.

He sought out a bathroom and locked himself in a cubicle. He got out a small, wireless earpiece and placed it in his ear, affixed a union jack pin to his lapel and flipped a switch to activate it. He took out a pair of clear glasses from his pocket, slipped them on and switched on the wireless transmitter on the back of his belt buckle.

A pause.

Scarlet's voice: *'We have eyes. Confirm audio.'*

He whispered into his lapel. 'Confirm.'

*'Audio confirmed our end too. But resist the temptation to lift the mike to your mouth and for God's sake don't push the earpiece into your ear either, dead giveaways.'*

'Got it.'

*'That's okay, that's why we're doing this today, to get you used to it. Go and check in the mirror that the earpiece isn't visible. We'll use a codename from now on.'*

'Oh? What is it?' His stupid thought about Nighthawk popped back into his head. It wasn't much better.

*'Seagull.'*

He could hear her smile as she said it. 'Bloody Palace fans.'

*'I'll step back now and hand you over. Good luck.'*

He flushed the toilet, went out to the basins and angled his head to look in the mirror.

*'Looks good to me tío. Seagull ... sorry.'*

It was good to hear Dante's voice. Thank God he'd not been paired with Drew, he could only imagine the snide comments he'd have to deal with.

*'Please use our agreed gestures and only talk if we are definitely alone.'* All business now. Ocean brushed his fingers against his forehead to acknowledge. Time to get to work.

At staff reception Ocean asked for Andrea. A few minutes later, a short officious woman in a blazer and skirt of the dark green and purple Wimbledon colours appeared with a walkie-talkie in palm.

'Stuart?'

'That's me,' he offered his hand. 'Stuart Thompson.' *Well, at least it wasn't Smith.*

'Well we're really pleased you could fill in for Matty for the last couple of days of the tournament at such short notice.'

'What happened to him?'

She screwed up her nose. 'Food poisoning I think.'

'Poor guy.'

'You a big tennis fan?'

'Yeah, I'm a massive tennis head.'

'O-kay then,' Andrea laughed, 'so let me run through what we need you to do.'

It took about ten minutes to explain his duties and although Scarlet had given him an overview, Ocean still couldn't believe that this was a real job. His employer was the anti-doping arm of the International Tennis Federation. The ITF selected players for drug tests at random and when they did, sent a medical professional to collect blood and urine samples. Ocean's 'job' was to accompany both medic and player to independently observe the sample collections, guarding against any possible collusion between player and medic. But what really got him was that he would have to watch (properly watch) the urine sample being produced. In short, Ocean was being paid to stare at the privates of Wimbledon tennis players. Thank God Drew didn't know.

Ocean covered Centre Court and Court One. The penultimate day of Wimbledon offered few matches, but they were important ones. On Centre there were three finals: the Women's Singles, Gentleman's Doubles and Women's Doubles whilst Court One hosted the Invitationals and the Juniors.

Furnished with an order of play and a walkie-talkie, Ocean decided to walk off his coffee buzz and run some reconnaissance. First, the taxi rank outside Gate 7 on Church Road where he'd seen Matty the night before; the bus stop right outside Gate 3; the car parks off Somerset Road and which exits corresponded closest to Southfields, Wimbledon Park and Wimbledon stations. His earpiece crackled.

*'Bien. Now familiarise yourself inside Centre.'* Dante and Scarlet had been silent for so long he had almost forgotten they were there. Ocean acknowledged. Inside the bowels of Centre, Ocean wandered around the tidy chaos. A badger-like TV presenter he recognised walked briskly down the corridor, he tried to recall his name.

*'Apparently that's John Inverdale. And you should stop staring.'*

Ocean resisted the urge to laugh and switched his attention to a female player in bright white tracksuit top, huge tennis bag resting on her shoulder.

*'Sabrina Connolleyi. Women's finalist.'*

It was like having your own personal mind reader ready to tell you everything you wanted—or didn't want to know. He paced down the corridor, seeing the large press conference room set out in cinema style seating and stuck his head in. A technician was fiddling with a bunch of microphones sprouting like black flowers from the table. A few people, journalists he guessed, were bent over their phones and tablets tapping feverishly. After the big games this place would swell with journos, and one in particular. His mark. Slater.

Further along the corridor he found the medical treatment room where the drug testing would take place. Stairs led up to restaurants, the smell drifting down was warm and gravy like. So much for the sweet summer smells of Pimms, strawberries and cream. It made him think of Mum, she would probably be at home planning another tennis party for tomorrow. He owed her a call, why did he keep forgetting?

His ears pricked up. There was a commotion in the lobby.

*'See what's going on.'*

Ocean sidled into the lobby and leant against the wall, pretending to text while a small group of journalists surrounded a smartly dressed elderly man. His thinning grey hair was combed in a side parting and he wore a tie of the club colours over a white shirt, cream chinos and brown leather shoes.

'Now look,' he said, 'I don't really think this warrants further discussion. The tournament is almost over. The vote is next week and I will soon be returning to my office, fighting the good fight.'

Something locked into place. This was Lord Cloudsley, the Chair of the All England Club and Labour peer. There'd been some controversy about a vote on a resolution or something, Ocean couldn't really remember. He cursed his laziness at not paying more attention to the article in the paper.

The reporters held their phones out inches from Lord Cloudsley's chin, using them as recording devices: 'If the resolution gets ratified by parliament next week, would you consider resigning?'

'I advocate diplomacy above all else. I will continue to oppose any resolution that involves arming anyone, be they religiously motivated rebels or teletubbies.'

'But will you resign?' the reporter insisted. Ocean realised Cloudsley had dodged the question without him even realising. But of course, politicians must be ninja at Neuro-Linguistic Programming.

'Whether it passes or not is down to the moral courage of the MPs who vote, not on whether or not I happen to have a secondary role at the world's most prestigious tennis tournament.'

*'Er ... Seagull? She says to move on, scope out the press hospitality area.'*

This felt important. It was news and where there was news there would be journalists. Why would Scarlet want him to move ... unless ... two wriggling thought strands met and made a possible connection. Was Cloudsley the politician caught up in Slater's phone hack? The codenamed Joe?

He gestured acknowledgement, wishing that Scarlet wasn't listening so he could find a quiet spot and confide his suspicions to his friend. Before he could take a step, his radio came to life.

'Stuart?'

'Here in Centre, over,' he said into the equipment.

There was a pause. 'Great. Head to the men's dressing room, they're going to test Melo. He's in the men's doubles final today. He's Brazilian.'

Let's hope he doesn't *have* a Brazilian, Ocean thought. 'On my way.'

Ocean observed the tests, first the blood—because Melo didn't quite need to go just yet. Then, with embarrassment he watched the urine sample. He was surprised how matter of fact both the medic and the player were, but then, they must have done it a hundred times before and to them it must just seem routine.

'*Tenho uns tomates do caraças.*'

Melo was talking to him with a cheeky grin on his face.

'Huh?'

'Means big balls,' he cracked an infectious smile.

'Well. Good luck!'

'*Obrigado irmão.*'

The medic screwed a lid on the sample.

'Don't go drinking that,' Melo said.

The medic smiled. 'Don't worry, I won't. Stuart? Ready to do the paperwork with me?'

Afterwards, Ocean grabbed a veggie burger and watched a bit of the doubles on the big screen. He would check out the press hospitality area later, then there wasn't much more he could do without Slater on site. He wished he were back practicing his picks and sleight of hand on Dante.

'*Seagull. I'm just going to grab us some sandwiches and coffee. I'll leave you with her.*' Dante said.

Ocean brushed his forehead, took another bite of burger just as Melo and his partner lost the first set. Shame. In his pocket, his phone buzzed. He didn't recognise the number.

'Hello?'

'It's Claude. Pretend it's your mother.'

The burger stuck in his throat. Claude sounded panicked. Ocean cough-swallowed. 'Oh, hey Mum.'

'Can Orca hear you?'

'One sec,' Ocean lowered the phone and took a few steps away from the crowd. 'Hey,' he whispered to Scarlet, 'I'm getting really bad feedback, it's just my Mum. Mind if I take it?'

'*Be quick.*'

Ocean disabled the transmitter and pressed the phone to his ear.

'Claude?'

'Are we alone?'

'Yes.'

'You're sure nobody can hear you right now?'

Ocean was spooked by his tone. Warren could hack phones and listen to conversations but what could Claude be so worried about?

'I can't be sure.'

'*Merde.*'

'What's this about?'

'I ... I'm worried they will hear it.'

An idea struck him. 'Claude. Try speaking in simple French. Let's see what an A in GCSE French is really worth.'

'Okay. I speak slow,' his friend took a breath, *'Je marchais dans les bois.'*

Ocean ordered the words into English in his mind. I was walking in the woods.

*'Il y avait un son bizarre et je suis allé jeter un oeil.'*

Something about hearing a strange sound and going to take a look.

*'J'ai vu un chien, rognant quelque chose.'*

I saw a dog and ... something, Ocean didn't know that word but didn't want to interrupt.

*'Quand je me suis rapproché, j'ai vu que c'était une main.'*

When I got closer I saw that it was a hand. So there was a dog doing something to a hand?

*'J'ai fait fuir le chien.'*

I chased the dog away.

*J'ai creusé la terre.*

142

I dug up the earth.

*C'était le corps de Vasile.'*

Ocean's heart went cold. Vasile? But they'd all watched him go in a taxi?

*'Que dois—je faire?'* Hysteria returned to Claude's voice. What should I do?

# 20

## DILEMMA

'Claude, tell me you're joking!'

'I'm scared Ocean!'

Thoughts swarmed like plankton carried on a current.

'What will they do to me if they find out I know?' Claude sounded in no doubt about who he thought had killed Vasile. But none of this made any sense. Orca had a single-minded goal. No more war. There was no way he could draw a line from that aim to Vasile being killed... he stopped in sudden realisation. Of course. There was a reason this didn't make sense.

It wasn't true.

It was just another test. A test of his loyalty to Orca. The more he thought about it, the more it made sense, even in the ludicrous scenario of Orca killing Vasile, would they really just bury him in the woods? No. Of course not. Claude had been put up to this phone call and now Ocean had to be doubly careful of what he said.

'Claude? We should trust Orca.'

'What?'

'Just act normal. I'm on a mission right now.'

'But what about Vasile? He's dead Ocean! He's rotting in that wood!' all pretence of speaking in code had long been chucked out the window.

'I understand,' Ocean said coolly. Claude was good, almost convincing. Damn Scarlet and her lying classes. He would appease Claude with logic for now. 'Claude, think about it. If Vasile really is dead it's because he knew too much about something. If you run away, they could do the same to you.'

'What do you mean, "If Vasile really is dead!" You don't believe me?'

'No, it's not that.'

'Why would I make up something like this?' Claude sounded hurt but it was exactly what Ocean would say if he were trying to force a lie through. Appeal to the subject's emotions.

'What I'm saying makes sense Claude. Play the game. Don't give them a reason to hurt you and it'll buy us some time to figure all this out okay?'

There was a pause. 'Maybe...'

'Sit tight. Let me look into it. It'll be alright.' He hung up. Well that was weird. At least he hoped it was weird. The other option was too frightening to consider.

He kicked off his shoes and heeled the door shut.

'Hey, I brought you a latte Scarlet.'

'I *am* training you well aren't I?'

They were huddled around the computer.

'Eh, tío. It was good today, no? You ready for tomorrow?'

'I'd like to practice a few picks on you later, but mostly yeah.'

'Good idea,' said Scarlet, 'what does Mike say? Practice, practice, practice?'

'Yep. But right now I can't think any further than my stomach. I'm craving a pizza. There's a spot down the street that looks good.'

Scarlet nodded to the tablet. 'Order me something. No anchovies though. Or ham and pineapple, horrible combination.'

'Actually, I might walk over and pick it up myself. Either of you want to come along for a walk?'

Dante rubbed his face and sighed. 'You know what? My brain is like fried eggs. I need a break from the screen. Might do us good, Scarlet?'

She shook her head. 'You go. I need to update Frank on today anyway. Keep your chatter tight in public.'

So far so good, Ocean thought. He waited for the lift doors to close and told Dante about his call from Claude.

'*Dios mío,* and you really think it was a test?'

'I think so. But I don't know for sure.' The doors split and they headed through the lobby and onto the street. 'Can you do some digging?'

'How can I? Scarlet's always there watching.'

'Bloody hell. I feel terrible not believing Claude. We need to check.'

'If I was on my own I'd get the airline manifests for that day, see if Vasile got on that plane to Bucharest. With his mobile number I could find out more. Failing that I can always try and mine the Orca servers....'

They entered the pizza place and ordered a large *Diavola* to share and a small *Primavera* for Scarlet.

'I need to get some time on my own.'

'She must take loo breaks though right? She's not a robot.'

'Yeah, but only for a few minutes.'

Ocean leant on the counter, thinking. Baking pizza dough and melting cheese wafted into his nostrils, he really had to stop thinking about his stomach and focus on the matter at hand. The solution was simple.

'Wait here, I'll be back in two minutes.'

Ocean dashed out and immediately saw what he was looking for. Got to love London for that. He jogged over to the illuminated green cross with digital clock underneath.

When he got back to the pizza place, Dante had two cardboard boxes loaded on top of each other. Ocean stuffed a pharmacy bag in Dante's pocket.

'What's that?'

'Laxative drops.'

Dante's face lit up. 'For the latte? Let's Matty Adams that bitch!'

Ocean laughed. 'Exactly. Got to be some perks to being the coffee boy right? Let's hope it buys you enough time.'

'Come on *tío*, let's hurry or she'll get suspicious.'

In the confines of the lift, the amazing pizza smell intensified and Ocean had to force himself to think just a bit longer.

'Dante ... If something goes wrong tomorrow, maybe we should have a code word.'

'For an emergency?'

'Just as a precaution. So you can signal me without her knowing.'

'And then what?'

'We split, go to ground.' Ocean nearly laughed. 'I've got a feeling we will look back at this and laugh at ourselves for being the two most paranoid losers in the universe.'

147

'Or not,' Dante replied guardedly. 'The code word?'

That at least was easy. 'Rocky.'

# 21

# THE PICK

The clock hit the hour. A security guard unclipped the cordon, and the Wimbledon crowd surged forth; the body-painted, the sun-burnt; the straw-boatered; the kilted; the banner-wielding; the nervous and the hopeful. The tide flowed for Centre Court and Harper Hill.

From the second floor of Centre Court stadium Ocean shook his head at the crowd's brisk walk. Their sheer restraint, clearly wanting to run to get the best viewing positions. *Let go*, he thought. *Run.* What was wrong with unabashedly striving for things?

Outside press hospitality, the corridor was stuffy: the glass façade created a greenhouse effect that outwrestled the air con. He eased his collar. Amidst the hullaballoo of final's day and the confusion about Vasile, Ocean had a job to do. His mission. All else would have to wait.

A security goon had the entrance to press hospitality covered. He was the meticulous type, furrowing his brow at each pass, eyes darting from pass to face before allowing entrance. *Just my luck.* The press had long been admitted before the general public. Most of the hacks had phones pressed between ear and neck while they typed away on laptops. He had to get in.

Slater was inside. He was so much like the photo Ocean had seen, he might have just stepped out of it. The suit was the same, the hair pinned back by sunglasses and stubble so neat it looked the guy smeared it on with the flat of a knife. Slater obviously had no qualms about drinking on the job. Despite the jugs of orange juice, the guy had a glass of champagne in his left mitt and it wasn't even midday. Good. A bit of booze might blunt the guy's senses and make him easier to pick.

Slater tapped away at a white iPhone with his right hand; the same model Ocean had practiced fitting the bug in. Right-handed then. Logic followed that he probably kept his phone in his right-hand trouser pocket or his inner jacket pocket.

*'Don't stay there too long tío. Hovering outside the press hospitality is only going to draw attention.'*

Acknowledge. Ocean took a step and froze. Slater's phone was ringing. The journalist tabled his glass, stuck a finger in his ear and joined Ocean in the corridor.

'What! Hold on mate, I can't hear you.' Slater barged past. Ocean's heart quickened its beat, but Slater didn't even look at him. Why would he?

Ocean tiptoed behind. Might he have an opportunity right away?

'Yeah?' Slater listened for a few seconds. 'I don't think I'll have time.' Another pause. 'Well that depends how long the final goes on for,' he looked up at the ceiling. 'Yes, I'm interviewing him *after* the ceremony and the handshakes. That's if the old codger's got any energy left.'

The chairman would hand the trophies to the finalists. Slater was talking about Cloudsley, Ocean was sure of it. He had to calm himself, focus on the pick but his heart was thumping so loud it was a wonder that Slater didn't down his phone and yell at Ocean to keep it down over there, he was trying to talk! Ocean stilled his breath. Window: dark green colour of the Wimbledon walls. Ambling spectators. Bright hanging baskets. Inside: Slater's pin-striped back. The tang of sweat masked by too much cologne.

'I can, but it'll be tight. Let's call it after I've spoken to him. Doubt he'll give me anything juicy but like you say, I can probably write half of it now, background piece on the events so far, speculate on a resignation and just top it up later. Yeah, cool. That should give the subs enough time before the deadline.'

Slater slipped the phone in his jacket pocket. Ocean was getting good at this. A step. He was right behind Slater. Calm. Hands up, ready. He visualised the move. Slater turned and bumped clumsily into Ocean.

'Wow, sorry there mate.'

Ocean brushed down his suit. No eye contact. 'No harm done.'

Only when he was round the corner did he pad his sleeve. Yes! There it was, the hump of phone under the sleeve fabric. Now he had to be quick. Slater would check his phone every minute at least. He'd think back to bumping into that kid in the corridor for sure.

'Nice pick Seagull, your nearest toilet is behind you, yes that's it, next right. There you go.'

There was a free cubicle. He lowered the lid, placed the phone on the surface, kneeled down and got out the miniature

151

screwdriver disguised as a key ring. Sweaty palms. He did the screws fast and prised open the case. He levered up the battery, popped it out, slid the bug in place, replaced the battery and clipped the case back shut. The screws eluded his fingers for a moment, dancing around the toilet lid. He gripped one, screwed it in, then the other. Ten seconds it wasn't, but he just hoped it was fast enough.

*'Hit lost property quick, down the stairs, second right.'*

He was glad Dante had a map open to guide him. He'd memorised most of the routes but under pressure it was easy to forget.

*'Seagull, I have the mark. He's outside hospitality, looking on the floor for his phone. Hurry up.'*

Bloody hell, it was less time than he'd imagined. He ran down the stairs two at a time and held his walkie-talkie up as he approached the Lost Property desk.

'Really sorry, in a massive rush,' and pointed at his walkie-talkie. 'Found this phone outside press hospitality on the floor. Probably belongs to a journo, would you mind logging it or whatever?' he slid the phone on the desk.

The lady pointed at a form and opened her mouth to speak.

'Sorry! I really do have to run.' Ocean ignored her weak call for him to come back.

*'Really good!'* Dante was excited. *'Get outside and away from the mark—he's heading down the stairs now!'*

Ocean stepped through the automatic doors into the warm sunlight, blinking like an owl, barely containing the urge to do a little celebration dance on the spot.

That. Was. Awesome.

He flowed with the crowd to Harper Hill. The final must be starting soon. He was pumped; he couldn't believe how well the plan had gone. He *was* made for this stuff after all.

'*The mark is talking to Lost Property and pointing upstairs.*'

Come on you bugger. Give him back the phone.

'*The mark has the package. Repeat, the mark has the package. Congratulations Seagull.*'

He pumped his fist; he didn't care if the crowd thought he was a weirdo.

'*Hold tight.*' It was Scarlet, '*I want to run some tests to check for functionality. Seagull remain on standby.*'

He acknowledged and overheard some faint chatter between them. She was sending Dante out to get their lunch. Of course. Dante had his own mission to complete; the exhilaration of his success waned a little. Soon they'd learn that all this business with Claude was all some stupid test, that this was his future. How long did those laxative drops take to kick in anyway?

His radio crackled. 'Stuart?'

Urgh. He'd forgotten he had a *real* job to do too. He considered ignoring it but thought better of it. 'Yes?'

'Can you get over to Court One please, they want to test one of the juniors.'

'On my way.'

When Ocean got to Court One a few minutes later, the player wasn't there. The medic checked his watch every thirty seconds, sighing each time. A man in a suit popped his head round the door to say the junior had been mid-interview with an Italian newspaper and was hurrying over. The medic was stony-faced.

'*It's me. She's in the bathroom.*' Dante came in. Ocean straightened up, ready to hear Dante's news. He gestured that he was ready.

Then the Italian junior burst through the door in a flurry of panic.

'So sorry! *Scusi, scusi!*'

Dante was talking into the earpiece but Ocean couldn't grasp any of the words. *Shut up!* He wanted to yell, but the Italian was practically yelling his apology. All Ocean could do was gesture for a problem. Dante stopped talking.

'If you make the pro-circuit and turn up this late for a test, you'll be labelled a drug cheat even if you're clean!' the medic retorted.

Ocean dug his nails into his arm, willing them to dial it down so he could hear Dante. And finally, when the reprimanding and the apologising ceased, he gave the acknowledgment gesture.

'*We've got a major problem tío!*' Dante's voice lowered to a whisper. '*That's the bathroom! I think she's ...*'

It went silent. Ocean, lock-jawed, stared at the needle hitting the Italian's vein. A tide of dark blood rose in the syringe. A major problem ... Did that mean Claude was telling the truth about Vasile? Tentacles of an unknown dread reached and lurched within him, looking for purchase in the wall of his guts. He fought down the nausea and waited and prayed for Dante to speak again, to tell him that it was a joke, that really everything was okay.

# 22

# THE NEWS

O cean shot through the paperwork. Surely it couldn't be *that* bad could it? After all, Dante hadn't said their code word... but then Scarlet hadn't been present. There was no call to use it. Christ, he had to find a spot to talk to Dante but everywhere he looked there were people. Finals day of a major tennis tournament was not the time or place for peace and solitude.

Away from the major showcourts, he passed a court with the nets down with maybe fifty plastic seats but there were still people dotted about sunbathing. He went to the next. Again there were a few people, just teenagers, but they were clustered down one end of the court. *Just teenagers*. How easy we are to dismiss.

With a wary eye, Ocean sat at the opposite end of the court.

'Guys? What's happening?' he whispered.

There was nothing.

'Guys?'

*'Sorry Seagull.'*

His heart sank. It was Scarlet.

*'I'm not feeling too hot. I've sent our friend to the pharmacy. Everything is good. The bug's operational. You can turn off your equipment. Head back here to base when your shift finishes.'*

'Understood,' he switched his transmitter off, removed the Union Jack pin and rammed his glasses into his pockets. What the hell was going on? He checked his phone. Five missed calls and three messages. He slapped his palm to his forehead. Why hadn't he checked it?

Before he could open a message, the screen lit up with an incoming call.

'Hello?'

'*Tío* it's me!' Dante was out of breath.

'Where are you?'

'On the street outside the flat, Scarlet sent me for some meds. I think she suspects something! I've been trying to get you for—'

'Never mind that. What the hell is going on?'

Dante took a breath. 'Vasile didn't catch his flight home. His phone's dead.'

'Oh God,' Ocean felt like he was melting, why hadn't he believed Claude?'

'Ocean, it gets worse,' he could hear Dante's voice breaking like he might cry. 'What have we done?'

'What do you mean?'

'The mission! I found emails between Orca and the client.'

'The politician? This "Joe" person. Is it Lord Cloudsley?'

'What? No. They lied to us! The client isn't a politician at all! It's a lobbying group for a weapons manufacturer.'

Ocean was struck dumb for a moment. Cogs turned and steamed in his head. Why would a weapons manufacturer want him to plant a bug in a reporter's phone?

'Wh—I can't process this. So that whole story about Joe is completely made up?'

'More than Disney. But there's more.'

This couldn't get any worse, could it?

Dante's voice shivered as he spoke, low and slow: 'The bug you fitted in that reporter's phone. It wasn't no bug.'

With horror, the cogs finally locked into place in Ocean's mind:

Lord Cloudsley was campaigning against the sale of millions of pounds worth of weapons from Britain to the Middle East in a vote next week. Ocean had installed a device into Kenny Slater's phone on behalf of a weapon manufacturer. Kenny Slater was interviewing Lord Cloudsley after the final.

Dante's words confirmed what he now already knew.

'It's no bug. It's a bomb.'

# 23

# ROCKY

It came in a torrent, unstoppable as it was disgusting. He barely had time to shuffle his feet wide enough before the vomit splattered and covered the floor. What a fool he'd been. How trusting. How ignorant. And the sickness he felt was nothing compared to the disgust he felt towards his uncle and father. Stopping war? How could he have been so gullible to believe that?

He couldn't process it. Weapons sales to war-torn states? Murdering Vasile? All he could think of was the reporters in the lobby, holding their phones aloft to record Cloudsley's comments. He spat bile out of his mouth.

*We move in silence and shadow. Our work is only done when nobody knows it is us who has done it.*

Kenny Slater was nothing but a catspaw. An unwitting suicide bomber.

*By shadow we craft a future of our own making.*

'Ocean! Are you there?'

He zoned back to the present. His phone sat cradled in his lap.

'Yeah,' he wheezed. The taste in his mouth was awful. 'I'm here.'

'What the hell do we do? I'm freaking out.'

Turn back time. Erase the last few hours, no, the last few weeks of their existence. He had no idea.

'Oh God,' he gasped, 'does Scarlet know that we've worked it out?'

'I don't know *tío*. She's acting funny but then that might be those drops I put ... oh my god.'

'What?'

He could hear traffic in the background.

'A black Mustang just went past.'

'What!'

'It's pulled up outside the safe house. It's him! It's Frank! He's going up into the block.'

'Frank's in London?' Ocean tugged at his fringe. 'Get out of there Dante! This is a Rocky situation. Do not go back up there!'

'Okay *tío*.' Dante's voice jolted, he was running already. 'I'm heading for the tube. I'll ditch the phone, go invisible.'

'Go! Find a way to contact Claude securely, tell him to split.'

'And the others? Drew and Kaya?'

'I don't trust them.'

'Good luck Ocean. Get out of there too, fast. To get in touch use a message board for Cádiz football club fans okay? I'll find you.'

'*Suerte hermano*.' Ocean hung up.

What was Frank doing here? Ocean stepped over the puddle of sick and ran from the court.

He had to think. He knew next to nothing about the device he'd implanted in Slater's phone. Logic was his only weapon. The device was slim, so the explosion would probably be small and localised, relying on Slater's proximity to Cloudsley. He could rule out a timed explosion; nobody could know exactly when the interview would take place. Which left a remote detonation triggered by a phone call. But how would Scarlet know precisely when to call?

His head was so overloaded and his feet were running so fast towards Centre that he almost didn't believe it when he heard his name. He paused, disbelieving, and heard it again. Clearer now.

'Ocean? O? It is you!'

The voice was familiar and took a second to place; it had been weeks. As he turned, a cocktail of warm familiarity, shame, dread and disappointment did the rounds of his body and were confirmed when he saw that berry brown, confused face.

'Andy?'

As if saying his name aloud might turn him into a mirage. It didn't.

'Bloody hell, didn't expect to see you here.' Andy wore a Wimbledon T-shirt and had a pint slopping over his hand.

'Likewise.'

Ocean's mind sprinted ahead, concocting various explanations for why he was there and why he hadn't had time to ring.

'Well done for your exams you little Einstein.' Andy took out a pack of nicotine gum, popped one in his mouth and chewed.

'Thanks ...'

'Skye's just in the ... oh, there she is.'

'Ocean?' Mum, in a matching T-shirt, squinted at him as if he weren't real. Her face lit up. 'Ocean!'

160

'Hi Mum.'

A warm hug. A peck on the cheek. He considered falling to his knees in tears and telling them everything or just running away. But what he actually did was worse; he stared dumbly at them, paralysed by the knowledge that he was about to kill at least two people and had no idea how he could stop it.

'Are you feeling alright, honey? You're a bit pale.'

He loosened his collar with his fingers. 'Not really ... I—'

'Harper's two sets up! Markovic is on the ropes now! Don't think you need to be feeling any nerves O.' Andy said.

Two sets up! If he won the third then that would be it. How long did a set last? Half an hour? More? Then the Slater-Cloudsley interview would take place and boom ... he would become a killer. No. A terrorist.

He had to deal with this problem as coolly as any other. The quickest way to get out of their company was to wade through it.

'I didn't know you'd be here,' he said as conversationally as he could.

'We didn't either, your mum persuaded me to queue from midnight last night just to watch it on the hill.'

'Damned if I was going to miss it and not be able to say that I was there! And how about you mister? I thought this job of yours was in Leicester?'

Ocean rolled out a story; something garbled about one of Benny's friends needing some fill in staff for the last few days of Wimbledon. It all being a mad, mad rush and not having the time to sleep, let alone call. He glanced at his phone. He had a new message from Dante. 'I better get back to work.'

'Ocean honey,' Mum placed a hand on his chest. Her breath was sweet, she'd been drinking. 'It must be fate that we bumped into you. We've got a bit of news that I wouldn't have wanted to share over the phone.' She lifted her hand and pointed at her fourth finger where an oversized diamond had barnacled itself to her joint. No way was this happening now.

'Oh wow,' his mouth was dry, it sounded fake so he tried harder, 'that's really, just, brilliant news guys. The best.' He embraced them each in turn. Wade on, wade on, wade through the thickening quagmire of crap. 'Congratulations guys.'

'Thanks mate. Join us for a drink later? We'll probably be at the Northcote. I can tell you how I popped the question, ' he said with a wink. At that moment a roar of applause went up from the stadium and Harper Hill. 'Should be a double celebration by the sounds of it.'

Ocean let a few more grains of time slip between his fingers and forced a smile. 'That'd be just … great. I've got to run but I'll call you later. You'd better get back to the match, don't want to miss history in the making!' he was sounding hysterical now and they looked at him with puzzled expressions. Maybe they'd put it down to news of the engagement. Whatever. He didn't care. He just needed to get away. Time was running out.

# 24

# FINAL

BBC One: sunrays splinter through clouds. London in miniature. The worm of the Thames, the BT Tower, Big Ben, the Wheel and the Gherkin are faded with haze. The Shard threatens to puncture the sky. Jump cut to an image of a blimp and then back to the panorama. The camera pans down, showing the Wimbledon grounds in relation to the rest of London. Centre and Court One are big mismatched eyes; the other courts form part of a bright green patchwork quilt with people making up the seams. Cut to a mid-shot of Harper's Hill. A couple of thousand people jump up, shaking cups and waving their hands. Signs are thrust aloft. *'Go Max!'* says one. *'Harper's Sharper!'* another.

Cut to inside Centre. Courtside. People mill back to their seats from the bar or toilet trips. The court is pale green, fading to a brownish yellow around the baseline. A pigeon flies across the court and lands on the lip of the roof. A ball boy replenishes a fridge with bottles while a ball girl carries towels and umbrellas. Close up on Max Harper, changing his sweaty shirt. Someone wolf-whistles in the crowd. Markovic stares into space. Close up on an attractive girl in the crowd. Close up of famous actors in matching blue suits and sunglasses. The

Prime Minister. The Beckhams. The players' enclosure. Cut to a close up of the Duke of Kent sitting next to Lord Cloudsley.

The umpire calls time. Centre Court erupts in a deafening cheer of applause. The camera changes to a shot of the yellow-lettered scoreboard, showing Harper leading the third set. Cut to Harper tossing his towel to the ball girl, then beating the strings of his racket against his wrist. Once, twice. A bounce of the feet to show he's ready.

Paralysed with indecision, Ocean watched all this on one of the wall-mounted TVs in the arteries of Centre. If only he knew how long the match would go on for. The police surely wouldn't believe him at first and would need time to check, to corroborate ... was there time for all that with Harper already ahead in the third? Ocean squinted at the screen and desperately searched the faces in the crowd for Slater. It was no use.

His phone buzzed in his pocket. Scarlet. His heart thumped like a drum. He had to answer it.

'Hi.'

'Have you heard from Dante?' Her tone was unreadable.

'No. Isn't he with you?' he said, hoping against hope that his voice wouldn't betray him.

'I sent him out a good half hour ago and he's still not back.'

'Maybe he's gone to get some food? Is everything alright?'

There was a pause. He sensed Frank's presence in the background, a consultative glance or mouthed question.

'Fine. I'm sure he'll be back shortly. See you later.' The hang up was as clipped as her tone.

Was she feeling him out or giving him a chance to shop in his friend and stay loyal to Orca? The message icon showed there was an unread message from Dante. He'd been so distracted by seeing Mum and Andy that he'd forgotten all about it.

Our friend is safe. Last msg. Am losing phone. Do same.

Claude was okay. That at least made him feel an atom's worth better. Applause on the TV. Markovic finished off a game and bounded over for the next changeover. The players sat, rubbed their faces with towels and took long slugs from their bottles. Markovic had fought back and was now 3–2 up in the third. That was good. Perhaps if the Serbian could go on to win the set then Ocean would have time to bring in the police. Of all the people in the world, Markovic was suddenly an unlikely ally for him.

Ocean stuck his head in the press room. Empty. They would all be watching the game. Where though? Perhaps the journalists all sat together. A waitress was clearing a table of canapé-smudged trays and dirty glasses. There were a few people on phones, making use of the changeover and there, Ocean realised with a start, was Slater.

Automatically, he was inside. Slater slipped his phone into his pocket and headed for the courtside entrance. Just a few steps and—

'Where do you think you're going?' There was a hand on his chest. Ocean nearly yelped with the shock of it. The security goon. Where had he come from?

'Er ...' he said, buying time. 'I'm hungry. I saw canapés being cleared.'

The goon glanced down at his pass and nodded over to the table. 'Grab yourself one or two but then I want you out of here, this is press only and it's more than my job's worth.'

*More like a jobsworth*, Ocean thought. Just his dumb luck. He thanked the guy and for forms sake scooped up a couple of soggy smoked salmon and cream cheese blinis, stuffing one in his gob. His could still faintly taste vomit and the last thing he felt like doing was eating but he chowed it down anyway and eyed the court door.

The goon was still watching. 'Out!' he pointed.

Dashing for the court door and climbing over spectators to get to Slater was not a plan worthy of the name. Security would pin him down before he'd even get close. Back in the corridor he ran his hands through his hair and tugged at it until it hurt. He wanted to punch the window through. There was still time, perhaps more than he thought. He'd gotten through Orca's tests against tight time pressure hadn't he? And he'd learnt that if you can't think through a problem then you think around it.

Scarlet would only detonate the bomb when she knew Cloudsley and Slater were together ... which returned him to the question: how would she know when? He thought back to earlier in the day. Hadn't Dante given him a second-by-second update on Slater's movements to Lost Property? The security cameras!

A few paces down the corridor he found a camera tucked into the fold between ceiling and wall, too high to reach. It was trained on the Ladies and Gents toilet doors opposite and caught the traffic walking to and from the press hospitality area. Ocean stared into its black eye. Were Scarlet and Frank looking at him now?

He hid his face and followed the cable down the corridor. The game now was simple. Cut the camera feed and Scarlet would be blind and unable to risk detonating the bomb.

# 25

# CODE BLACK

The cables led through a set of double doors to another camera. Black milestones. He sensed Scarlet and Frank's eyes on him, a static menace akin to the tribal masks outside Frank's room. Head bowed, he pushed through more doors and found that here, the cable trail funnelled through a wall into a comms room. The end of the trail.

The room's entrance was secure with a card swiper and keypad. He pressed his face to the window, seeing with a sinking heart that there was a second security door. And beyond that, three security officials sat in front of a bank of screens passing around a box of donuts. What had he been thinking? This sort of plan took weeks of planning, resources and reconnaissance. Panic was smothering his judgement.

He couldn't get to Slater nor cut the camera feed. It was like some warped version of the school science experiment with the *papier mâché* volcano except Cloudsley was the baking soda, Slater was the vinegar and they had to be kept apart in order to *stop* the explosion. A crawling sickness writhed within his insides.

'Yes!' someone yelled, followed by feverish clapping. Ocean ran to the source of the sound, finding two security guards in a welfare area, yelling at a TV.

'Yes! Come on!'

On screen Harper pumped his fist; he'd hit a winner or served an ace or something. Then he saw the score and wanted the ground to swallow him up. Harper was 5–4 up, serving for the championship. 30–0 to the good. Oh God... he'd run out of time.

'He's going to do it! I'm sure of it!'

'He has to,' said the other guard, 'it's his destiny.'

Rooted to the spot, Ocean watched Harper win the next point to set up three championship points. But Markovic, with all of Ocean's will behind him, saved each one in turn. Ocean stared so hard it was like he was controlling the ball with telekinesis. Markovic won a break point. Harper doggedly saved it but Markovic won another. Then Harper saved that. Ocean felt like the game had been arranged to personally torment him. Markovic won a third break point. Come on now, this was it. Ocean got his phone out, made a deal with the cosmos that should Markovic win the break point, he would dial 999. Harper drove Markovic back into the corner, the Serbian threw out a middling lob which Harper dispatched into opposite side.

'Nyah!' Ocean roared at the TV.

One of the guards nudged the other and pointed at Ocean. 'He's living through every shot that one!'

Deuce. Ocean wrung his fingers through a tortuous rally ending with Markovic fluffing a volley into the net. Championship point Harper.

'This is it,' Ocean whispered.

'Let's hope so,' the guard said cheerfully, not registering the despair in Ocean's voice, 'my ticker can't take much more of this.'

Ocean found himself rocking a little unsteadily on his feet. He rested his hand on the wall. He heard the grunt of the serve, the pock of balls, a premature cheer from the crowd, then the clip of the ball hitting the net. The crowd erupted. The commentator screamed: 'He's done it!'

'Wahey!' The guards jumped up and down on the spot, hugging each other.

Ocean slid down the wall and placed his head in his hands. The fuse was lit and he still didn't have a plan.

The ceremony passed in a flash. Interviews, hugs and trophy brandishing. Lord Cloudsley was safely on the screen, chatting to the Duke of Kent in the background. Ocean gnawed at his knuckles and watched the reporters drain out of hospitality and hurry downstairs for the post-final conference. But not Slater.

Ocean waited a few minutes and peered in. Slater was typing furiously on his laptop. Maybe Ocean could just go up to him and—

'Out!' The security goon again.

God he'd never wanted to punch someone so much in his life. 'I am out! The match is ov—'

'Out!' he repeated. Furious, Ocean took a step back.

There was laughter. Down the corridor, Cloudsley, the other ingredient for the eruption, was striding towards him, a small entourage in tow. Slater snapped his laptop shut and joined Ocean in the corridor. Ocean was between the two men. Spying had failed. His plan had failed, the time for finesse, long passed. He had to act now.

Ocean dived into hospitality and grabbed a jug of orange juice.

'Hey!' the security goon yelled but Ocean was already back out. He flicked the liquid at the camera. It splattered against the lens and slopped in a slash down the wall.

'Security!' someone yelled.

'This lad's gone bonkers,' said Slater.

'Slater! Give me your phone, there's no time to explain.'

Slater looked at the phone in his hand and then at Ocean. 'How do you know my name?' His eyes narrowed. 'It's you again isn't it? You nicked my phone!'

There really was no time to explain. Ocean cocked his arm and jabbed Slater square in the nose. It exploded with a sickening crunch, blood bursting out through his nostrils. Ocean shook out his hand as Slater staggered back, cupping his hands over his nose, still gripping his phone somehow.

'Give it here,' Ocean said through clenched teeth and set about prising the phone from Slater's blood-slicked fingers.

'No,' Slater garbled.

But Ocean had it. Yes! Then there was a hand on his shoulder.

'Stop that! Calm it!' It was the goon, he had a firm grip. Ocean brought his elbow back as hard as he could and connected with the guard's groin.

'What on earth is going on here?' It was Cloudsley, striding towards them.

'Stay where you are!' Ocean screamed and for a second Cloudsley stopped, assessing Slater's bloody face and the security guard groaning on the floor.

'Young man!' Cloudsley bellowed.

171

## ORCA RISING

'Code black, press hospitality,' the security goon wheezed into his walkie-talkie.

Ocean gripped the blood-greased phone. The juiced security camera was trained right on him. Was Orca watching this? His phone vibrated. Scarlet. If he didn't pick up she'd ring Slater. Cloudsley took a step closer. Ocean knew it with certainty then.

He was about to die.

Out of the corner of his eye, the toilet door to the Ladies swung open. A reporter stepped out into the corridor and blinked in confusion as she surveyed the scene. Ocean dived for the door, squeezing in just before it could shut. It took less than a second to see that the cubicle doors were all open, the toilets empty. Blind luck. He tossed Slater's phone into the toilet bowl, spun on his heel and charged back out. Straight into the arms of the goon.

'Get down!' Ocean screamed, yanking them both to the floor.

Then the explosion ripped the afternoon in two.

# 26

# SIREN

I t was silent, creepily so. A mist of dust swirled like a ghostly gas. There was a groan. A cough. Ocean raised his head and checked he was all there. He was. His ears rang like cicadas. He shook his head, dust shifted loose but the noise didn't budge. He brushed bits of plaster and chips of porcelain off his suit. A siren sounded. Not the dinging alarm clock kind like at school, but a searing wail and a computerised voice.

'Please make your way calmly to the nearest Fire Exit.' Double bleep and repeat.

'Is everyone alright?' he yelled, getting to his feet.

The explosion was bigger than he'd thought possible for such a small charge. The door had blown clean off its hinges and split like a cracker. Bits of plaster, debris and porcelain shards covered the floor.

'Everybody alive?' He dared to hope, dared to think. Bodies twitched under the rubble. There was another cough. Ocean waved the dust from his eyes. The female reporter was on all fours. Next to her, Lord Cloudsley was stirring. Ocean stepped over the security guard. His chest rose and fell; he was breathing at least. Ocean rolled him into the recovery position and moved on to Slater. He too was alive, his hand still cupped over his bleeding nose and groaning. Relief. Pure, unadulterated relief. There was plenty of damage but nobody had died. Nobody had died! He had stopped it. He had stopped *them.*

Ocean stared into the eye of the security camera, brushed his suit down and gave Scarlet and Frank the middle finger. He doubted they could see him through the dust. Then, as he lowered his hand, a chill ran down his spine.

If they caught him, they'd kill him for this.

He had to get away, go to ground like Dante and Claude. Voices. Help was on its way. Ocean backpedalled and ducked down a fire exit to the floor below and joined a stream of panicked people rushing for the gates.

In minutes he was beyond the Wimbledon complex and being jostled down the pavement with a shoal of people.

'Network's down,' a man said, anxiety stretching his voice. 'Can anyone get 3G? Check the news?'

People shook their heads.

'Are we under attack again?' Someone asked.

'No way am I risking the tube, I'm walking.' Another mumbled.

Ocean wished he could put them at ease. On his own device he had no network. Perhaps that was good; Orca might not be able to trace him. Still, he knew he'd best ditch the phone, in fact he should have ditched it long before. Despite overloaded pavements, the road traffic continued to flow and he watched for a truck or open window to toss his phone into.

A buzzing in his fist. The triumphant theme music from Rocky. His phone. The surprise of it made him flinch.

Heads all turned to face him. 'What network you on mate?'

But Ocean couldn't answer. Though his feet still moved zombie-like with the crowd, his breath stuck in his throat at the sight of the name on the screen. Benny.

He pressed the phone to his ear. The connection opened.

'Orca are unforgiving creatures. Vicious, clever and wild.' Frank growled. The Mustang engine hummed in the background. Ocean looked around. There were people everywhere. He wasn't safe. He hunched down, kept moving.

'Too scared to speak are you? I might have known. Do you even realise what type of mistake you made today?' Frank's voice was barbed to puncture.

Still, Ocean couldn't speak.

'Well, do you?' Frank shouted.

'No,' he replied finally, in a small voice. His defiance in front of the security camera now a distant, petty memory.

'A lethal one.'

Ocean swallowed. Was he already in somebody's cross-hairs? Surely it was too crowded? He stooped lower.

'Lethal for you,' down the other end of the line, a siren passed in the background, 'and lethal for your family.' Frank cut the line dead.

Ocean stared at the phone. Mum. How could he have been so stupid? They'd get him where it hurt the most. The helplessness was molten, replete. He bit down on his fist and stifled the tears that threatened to come while the faint sound of a siren wailed.

He had to find her. Andy too. Frantically, he searched but there was no sign of them or those idiotic matching T-shirts, seemingly no chance at all in this hurried throng of bodies. Nausea returned. There was no longer a choice. He had to go to the police. He dialled the number. Nothing happened. His phone was jammed again.

'Argh!' he hurled it at the ground and watched in skitter under the heel of a stranger. What the hell could he do now? Flag down the police? That siren didn't seem to be getting any louder. The siren ...

He stopped. Listened. Was it the same one that he'd heard in the background when he'd spoken to Frank?

Ocean broke onto the road, earning a beep but got his head down and sprinted towards the sound. The traffic wasn't moving fast and at full speed he could almost keep pace with the car in front.

At last, he reached the blinking blue lights from an ambulance motorbike. A paramedic in green coveralls was kneeling, attending to someone on the curb. Ocean squinted up the road; there were two black cars but too many other vehicles obscuring his view to tell if one was the Mustang. Then, a double take at the paramedic. He was attending someone with a Wimbledon T-shirt.

Except this one wasn't white. The head was so red it was barely recognisable; the paramedic was trying to staunch the wound.

'Andy?'

'O?' Andy's voice was groggy and he wasn't quite looking in the right place.

'Do you know this man?' said the paramedic.

Ocean nodded. 'He's my ... my stepdad.'

'They took her O!' Andy wailed and pointed up the road. 'Someone took Skye!'

'You're going to be alright Andy. Just keep still and try and stay calm for me Andy.' The paramedic said.

For a second Ocean couldn't move. It was like someone had poured liquid nitrogen through his veins and frozen him inside out. They'd gotten to her already.

'Mum,' he mouthed. The next thing he knew he was straddling the paramedic's motorbike and kicking up the stand. He hit the ignition, twisted the throttle and shot up the road.

'Hey!'

Ocean weaved through the slow-moving traffic, the bike responded well, though it wasn't quite as easy to handle as the quad-bike. Sirens wailed. A fire engine, three police cars and two ambulances tore past, all heading for Wimbledon. Ocean overtook two cars, a bus and rounded a corner. The four stacks of Battersea Power Station appeared up ahead and with a tug at his hope, a black car on the horizon. He drew nearer. His heart sank. The car's insectoid shape gave it away as a modern SUV, not the Mustang. What if Frank had turned off already? This road meant driving deeper into London, surely that was a bad idea ... unless Frank was heading for the safe house?

Ocean twisted the throttle and jinked past the SUV and accelerated on, setting off the flash of a speed trap. He leant round a bend and there, six cars ahead he spotted the low-slung Mustang!

There wasn't a break in the traffic to overtake and Ocean revved and braked, stuck on the bumper of a car for what felt like an ice age.

'Come on, come on!' Up ahead there was a junction and Ocean watched in dismay as the black car shot through an amber light turning red. The train of cars in front slowed to a halt.

'Move! Get out of the way!' Ocean yelled, but it was lost to London's constant engine drone. The controls, there must be a horn to bash or some … no, he had something better—a siren. He twisted a knob and all at once the bike emitted a yelp. Blue lights flashed either side of the bike's windscreen. The cars ahead edged to the curb and Ocean squeezed to the front, waited a moment and then slipped into the passing traffic.

Though bulky, the bike was powerful and soon the wind was whipping past his ears and forcing his eyes to water horizontal streaks past his temples. In the growing list of things he wished he had: time, a weapon, he could now add a helmet with a visor. He was going too fast. But he had no choice. He couldn't lose Mum. He refused to.

The siren helped clear a path and within a mile he was on the bumper of the Mustang. The briefest joy he felt at having caught the car evaporated. With a growl the Mustang switched into the empty bus lane and accelerated away with incredible speed, opening up a new gap. Sirens had their uses, but subtlety wasn't one of them. Ocean switched it off and followed, keeping low on the bike to minimise wind resistance. The giant wheel: the London Eye appeared between gaps in the buildings. Waterloo? So they were heading east, not towards the safe house at all.

The Mustang took a sharp turn, wheels skidding and the back snaking round and disappeared into a tunnel. Ocean leaned into the corner sharply, gunned the throttle and shot in too. A bike passed the other way and then it was clear. Seeing his chance to pull level, Ocean pushed the bike harder. Orange ceiling lights streaked by. The high-pitched whine of his engine combined with the low growl of the Mustang made a deafening, guttural dial tone. He pulled level, risking a glimpse at the window, but all he could catch was the reflection of the sodium lights.

He gritted his teeth. Could he jump? Cling on to the roof and somehow get the door open? He inched the bike closer, readied his muscles and tested the distance. No. It would be suicide. But what about his suit jacket? If he could fling it onto the windscreen, it might obscure Frank's vision, force him to slow down. Ocean held on with one hand, feeling the bike wobble and inched his left arm out of his jacket. With a sudden jerk, the Mustang pitched sharply across his line and it was blind instinct that made Ocean squeeze the brake. As the bike slowed, the Mustang's bumper shaved his front wheel, the bike wavered and Ocean jammed his arm back through his suit jacket just in time to steady the bike. It held. Just.

Ocean exhaled. That was far, far too close. He'd been inches away from being squashed like a bug on the tunnel wall. Shaken, he exited the tunnel and into the sunlight. His elbows and knees twitched with the adrenaline, with fear.

It took all of Ocean's concentration to keep up. The Mustang ran red lights, slipped into bus lanes and took surprise turns. When it pulled off a daring two-car overtake, Ocean found himself further behind and unsure how long he could keep this chase up for. The fuel gauge read a quarter of a tank. How much did Frank have?

And then, on the horizon, there was a glimmer of hope. Tower Bridge was being raised. The first cars were coming to a standstill at the foot of the bridge. There were no turn-offs. No way out for Frank now.

The Mustang skidded to a stop beneath the shadow of the south tower. Two cars fell in behind. It was grid-lock. Frank, leapt out the driver's side and with a hand holding his Fedora in place slid over the bonnet and yanked Mum out the passenger side.

'Mum!' Ocean yelled, but he was still too far away. Her hands were bound behind her back. But she was moving at least, being pushed towards the bridge. Did he have a knife against her back? A gun? Ocean skidded to a stop and leapt from his seat. He rifled through the paramedic box on the back, desperately searching for something, anything that was weapon-like. There were scissors, a syringe. Not ideal, but he didn't have the luxury of choice.

Frank was pushing Mum to the entrance of the tower. Ocean pushed into his feet, wishing he had trainers instead of work shoes and sprinted after them. As he reached the Mustang, there was a blur of black. A metallic thud. Pain detonated in his right knee, the breath seemed to be sucked out of lungs and he was falling. Then the hot, graze of tarmac against his legs, his arms, his cheek.

'Whoo-ey!' the voice was exultant.

Ocean lifted his head. Blood dripped from his cheek onto the road. A second. Then the stinging came, deep as fire. Nearby, one of the Mustang's back doors had been snapped clean off its hinges. How had ... .

Drew stepped out from the doorless backseat and admired the hunk of metal lying on the floor.

'Just, wow.' The American shook his head.

Ocean pushed himself up onto his knees and buckled back down to the ground with pain. He tried again, trying his best not to let it show on his face and lifted his head.

Drew leant his neck to one side, then the other. 'Frank is gonna be pissed when he sees what you just did to his car. In fact, I'd say he'd kill you. Pity he'll be too late for a look in.' He cracked his knuckles. 'I've been looking forward to this a long time.'

180

# 27

# OUTWITTED

It was pathetic, but it was all he could think to do. Ocean scrambled under the Mustang, knee stinging as he rolled under the chassis. He'd never beaten Drew in a fair fight, let alone with so many injuries.

Drew laughed. 'You know I've never floored somebody with a car door before. That was a blast, but I gotta say I'm a little disappointed. I thought you'd at least be brave enough to fight! But then you were the chicken of the class weren't you?'

'Pretty much,' Ocean said to the metal tubes beneath the car. Through the letterbox of light between the chassis and the road, he saw the big American get down to his knees. 'I'd better drag your ass out here then. Make you fight like a real—'

Drew rested his hand on the tarmac and Ocean pounced, jabbing once, twice with the syringe. Drew snapped his hand back, breaking the needle off in his flesh.

'Ow! Dammit!'

*Too bad it was sterile*, Ocean thought as he tossed aside the syringe. With Drew's howls of pain as cover, he shuffled through to the other side of the car.

'Oh! You got me mad as a dog now! Come out and fight!'

Ocean kept going, scampering under a gardening truck now. He didn't have time for this. He didn't have time for anything. He ripped a strip from the bottom of his shirt with his teeth and tied it around the worst graze on his leg. The knot secure, Ocean crawled out the other side of the truck. He crouched low, wincing at the pain in his knee.

'Hey! What you doing?' the driver had an arm casually hanging out the window, a cigarette drooping from his mouth. The cigarette nearly fell from his open mouth as he took in Ocean's appearance.

'Blo-ody hell mate, are you alright? You look like a lawnmower's run over your face!'

Ocean pressed his finger to his lips and pointed at Drew. His aggressor was cradling his hand while furiously checking under cars and kicking bumpers in frustration.

'Should I call the police?' the man whispered.

'And the ambulance,' he said thinking of Mum, though he needed medical attention too, and so probably, did Drew.

'I'll tell 'em to hurry.' The driver reached for his phone.

Ocean peeked over the bonnet. Drew was turning around, desperately searching for him. 'What the hell! You trying to Viet Cong me you little jerk?'

Someone sounded a horn, a second joined in. The bridge was now up at full height. Ocean could see the approaching boat further down the Thames, still some way off yet. He crept to the next car, a small three-door he couldn't fit under, and so went on, drawing ever closer to the bridge. The tower wasn't far. He put some weight onto the knee and grimaced at the pain. No. He couldn't make a break for it. Drew would run him down in seconds.

Ocean picked a route back under the cars until he was near the Mustang again. He risked a glance. Drew was using the Mustang's boot for a step and climbed on top of the roof. Ocean dived to the floor, praying he was out of sight. His knee sang with the pain but he bit it down. Mum's life depended on it, and so did his own.

'Get back here!' Drew bellowed. Only horns sounded in response. 'Argh!' there was a thudding that sounded like Drew was beating his chest with his big gorilla arms.

More horns. Ocean slithered forward and heard Drew land heavily on the tarmac.

A glance up.

Drew was behind the Mustang, gazing down the road with a hand shading his eyes.

It was his chance.

Keeping low as a Cossack dancer, Ocean scrambled to the Mustang, eased open the passenger door and reached past the skull-headed gearshift. His fingers grasped the handbrake. He let it go. The car rolled backwards. One metre, two, then—

'What the—' A sickening crunch. The car jolted to a stop.

Drew was pinned between the bumper of the Mustang and the car behind, probably now with two broken legs. It was a move Vasile would have been proud of but Ocean felt no triumph.

The American's face had drained to the colour of the Thames.

'But—' Drew gasped, looking down in disbelief at his vice.

'There's an ambulance coming. You'll live.' Ocean said. 'Unfortunately.'

And without wasting another moment, he limp-ran to Tower Bridge.

A helicopter hovered like a gnat above the tower. Ocean hoped it was a news crew or even better, the police. But then a ladder dropped, unfurling twenty, thirty metres and swayed in the breeze. Orca. Ocean shielded his eyes. Nobody was on the upper walkway that connected the two towers. Not yet anyhow. He pushed his way through bodies and into the tower's glass-fronted lobby. There was a desk, cordoned-off stairs and in front of the lift, two staff members were trying to placate a swelling crowd of angry, ticket-wagging tourists. Some of the words fell to Ocean as he circled round the back of the group and ducked past the preoccupied staff.

'Sorry.'

'Incident.'

'Wimbledon.'

'Landmarks.'

'Lockdown.'

Ocean lifted his tender leg over the cordon. And didn't look back. The angry rancour behind him faded the higher he climbed, stair after stair. Fact boards adorning the walls headlined the history, statistics, the glass-bottomed walkway, the opening of the bridge and so on, up and up until his lungs wheezed and his calves burned.

Finally. The walkway. Ocean stopped dead in his tracks. It was eerily still and calm, like a stage had been set and the curtain drawn. Uncle Frank was in the middle, hands by his side. A cowboy waiting to draw. Beyond him, on the floor was Mum.

'Mum,' he gasped, gulping in air. She wriggled on the floor but couldn't seem to raise her head. 'What have you done to her?' His voice echoed over the beat-beat of the helicopter blades.

Frank cocked his head to one side. 'Made her more ... co-operative. But now she's served her purpose and lured you here, I guarantee that the next time I hit her, I'll do it until she stops twitching.'

Rage, purest white hot anger propelled him forward. He hid his limp, Mike Mysteryed the scissors from pocket to sleeve and... stopped.

'Lured?' he said.

'Lured.' Frank confirmed. 'We needed you silent as the grave.'

A trap? But there was the paramedic, the chase and even the timing of the boat coming through the bridge. No, it wasn't possible, shouldn't be possible ... but then he was here, wasn't he? And he'd not gone to the authorities.

He twisted around. Nobody there. No ambush. Did Frank have a gun? He calculated the gap between himself and his uncle—too far to dive. He took a small step nearer. He had to keep his uncle talking.

'Why are you doing this Uncle Frank?'

'Jesus kid, really? Where would I start?' he lifted a hand to count off on his fingers. 'You're an idiot, a cocky, arrogant thinks he knows-it-all moron who just harpooned his first operation in the most spectacular fashion because he doesn't understand the world.' Next finger. 'Because you know too much about Orca and third, because you're just as weak as your father. To be honest, I'm amazed you even managed to get past that knuckle-head Drew.'

Another step. 'But why don't you stop dancing around it and tell me what you really think?'

Frank threw his head back and let out a fake laugh. 'Ha! That's another thing. You think you're funny.'

'No. You're the comedian. Claiming your goal is to end war when all you want to do is murder people and support the arms trade!'

The smirk disappeared off Frank's face and he shook his head. 'Our goal *is* to end war. But how can there ever be peace where conflicting religious doctrines exist? The only way, the only path is to end it once and for all. A religious war, an all-out religious apocalypse.' Frank rose a fist and shook it, 'Arming the Buddhist bombers in Cambodia, inflaming the Christian right in the US, funding Islamic fundamentalism, stoking up hatred between Hindus and Muslims in Indonesia. We're the petrol being poured onto the flames! Only once it's all burnt to ash can we start again and base it on peace. Orca is the only organisation brave enough to see it. By shadow we craft a future of our own making.'

'Can you even hear yourself?' Ocean shouted and took another step forward. The gap now was only a few metres. 'You're insane!'

Frank shook his head. 'You see this is exactly the short-sighted, narrow-mind that got your Poppy killed. Well, that made me kill him.' He held up his hands. 'And yeah, yeah, if you hadn't worked that out by yourself then you're a bigger moron that I thought.'

Ocean's felt punched dumb.

'Oh you *are* that stupid? I've never even been to Bolivia in my life! What did I ever see in you? I blame myself, I really do, I wanted a successor, a legacy. I can't believe I was so foolish!'

Through the glass floor, Ocean caught movement below. The boat was passing through the bridge.

'And... she's clear! Well. Good talk Ocean. It's time for Skye to watch you die. But don't worry, I'll kill her too, that'll give me the whole set. An entire branch of Daley's wiped out! The *rotten* half of the tree.'

Ocean watched for an opening. His uncle glanced up at the helicopter. The rotators created a moving shadow on his cheek. There was a curl at the end of his mouth. A smile.

'No!' Ocean charged, pulling out the scissors.

It was on his second step that he heard it.

A bipping sound.

His ears roared. Glass shattered. And the floor gave way to nothing but air.

# 28

# FEDORA

Ocean threw out his arms, the scissors clattered against metal and something battered him in the side. He grappled air for something, anything, his desperate fingers catching, latching and yes! Something solid. A support strut. Glass pixels rained down as he desperately tried to secure his grip, suspended and swaying in the whipping wind as if clinging to the very sky itself.

Sudden pain. His ribs, God, his ribs! He must have landed on the metal struts on the way down. The pain was intense and the noise! Sensual overload; the rubbery underbeat of the chopper blades, the low whistle of the wind, the high note of more glass shards clinking against metal, the machine groan of the bridge's jaws closing beneath him; but most of all his breathing. He was exhaling so hard that his breath felt like it was coming out his ears. Then came a voice, shouting over it all.

'You may be predictable. You may be dumber than a bag of hammers. But you're a resilient little cockroach I'll grant you that.'

Ocean's arms burnt with the effort of holding on. Frank stepped to the edge, kicking glass into the hole. Ocean shielded his face and then up at his uncle, looming enormous as a mountain. His fingers were cramping, he gritted his teeth, held on with all of his waning strength.

'And what do we do with cockroaches? We squash them under our boots don't we?' Frank stamped down. Ocean instinctively let go and for a split second was suspended in the air, falling until he windmilled his other hand to a different spot on the strut. He grunted with the effort, grit his teeth and took in air just as Frank aimed another stamp. Ocean scampered, but too late, the boot catching the edge of his little finger. He held it, just. Grimacing at this new pain.

'Let's see how long you can monkey bar for.'

He couldn't last another attack. Ocean swung back, gathering his legs together to get momentum and let go, flying across to the next metal strut. He grasped it, the force of the movement made him feel like his ribs were tearing a hole in his side. If he could pull himself up, he'd be on the other side of the hole, away from Frank. He took a breath and tried to lift himself up. One inch, two ... then buckled. The pain in his side erupted and he almost let go completely.

'You can't even climb back up?' Frank shouted over the hole, clearly amused.

Ocean burned at him, this evil incarnate. His father's killer. The maker of murderers. He gritted his teeth in defiance. 'I wish Dad had killed you!'

Frank smirked at him. Then something strange happened. Ocean almost didn't believe his eyes. His uncle lurched forward, like a silent movie comedian pretending to fall—only he did—with arms flailing as he toppled forward into the hole.

## ORCA RISING

It took a split second to see the bound feet cocked in the air right in the spot where Frank had just been. Mum had kicked him off.

'Mum!' he yelled with joy.

Something tight gripped his ankles, yanking him down with the weight of an anvil. Impossible! His fingers cramped up again with the extra weight. He looked down. Frank held his ankles, clinging on for dear life.

'Mum!' he gasped, his fingers slipping from the metal.

And down he fell.

Wind rushed into his open mouth, flooding him before he could process it. Frank's hat shot up past him. Then he was pointing down, wind rippling his cheeks, just the bat shape of his uncle's black leather coat billowing below. The shrinking gap of water between the closing sides of the bridge. Could he make it? He remembered suddenly, some YouTube kid had jumped from the *lower* part of the bridge as a prank last summer, been knocked unconscious by the impact and nearly drowned.

Frank squeezed between the closing bridge. Giant pinball flippers they seemed all of a sudden, sent to crush. Ocean closed his eyes and waited for it to hit. The sun went. He opened them. A splash of white. Frank, exploding into the water. Ocean tried to get as straight as he could, hands over his head like the high divers on TV, arms squeezed against his ears. One last glance. Green w—

A deafening splash. Pain. Deep cold. And he was out.
Ocean was swimming a strong front crawl. Bubbles flowed past his goggles, formed where his hands broke the water and shovelled it back. Rhythm. Water slipping over skin. Music: deep bass notes of his kicking feet, the percussive slap and

splash of his hands and the high notes of sucking in air. One, two, three. Breath. One, two, three. Breath. It was unthinking. Mindless. Peaceful.

A glimpse of yellow.

So soon? He closed in, letting it grow larger in his goggles. Yes, this was it! He'd done it! He'd reached the yellow buoy.

He trod water, pulled his goggles onto his forehead and let out a whoop and tapped the buoy twice with his knuckles. Then, came Dad, his slovenly stroke hitting the water with its trademark clap. Dad stopped and rubbed his facemask up onto his forehead, revealing his brilliant blue eyes, his rare smile underneath.

'You did it! Look how far you've come.'

Shoreham beach was so far away, like a miniature model of itself. Ocean couldn't stop the smile creeping over his face, not because he'd finally reached the buoy, but because it had been so comfortable—he didn't even feel out of breath.

Dad's gaze dropped to the water. He squinted a second, slipped his mask down and plunged his face in. Rather than ask, Ocean lowered his goggles and sunk under too. He saw them immediately: those ghostly sea spirits with their tentacles dragging behind. Pulsating, throbbing towards them—too many to count.

He broke the surface.

Dad gripped him on the shoulder. 'We'll be fine O, don't panic. Just follow me, I'll find us a safe route back, just follow my kicking feet and the bubbles.'

Ocean nodded.

'Don't worry.'

'I'm not.' And he wasn't. Dad would steer him clear of harm. And so he swam, the pace a little tougher, the rhythm harder to establish, but he kept following the bubbles, occasionally catching sight of a big toe through the murk or the white of a jellyfish in his peripheral vision. And he kept going and going, following the trail of bubbles to safety on the shore.

Water exploded out from his lungs, the sky was moving too fast. No, it was the current. Tower Bridge. Hundreds of faces at the rail, shrinking away. Numbing cold. He wheezed in air. The pain in his side and knee were dulled but when he tried to make his arms move, something was wrong. With a tilt of the head he saw the grotesque angles of his arms, snapped like biscuits.

'Uh!' he tried to kick away from them like they weren't his. Panic was shortening his breath. The bank, where was the bank?

'Help!' he spluttered, swallowing more water but there was nobody to aid him and the Thames swept him effortlessly downriver. He twisted round to his side; the riverbank was some forty metres away. Calm down! Two-lengths of a pool was all. But he was fooling himself. It was more than that. The current was ferocious and his body broken.

On Tower Bridge he made out a speck in the walkway. Mum. He had to try. For her. For Dad. He took a gulp of air and plunged his head in. He wriggle-swam like a seal, relying on the rhythm of his legs, streamlining through the murky water. And was he imagining it? The path of bubbles? He kept going, following them, breaking the surface to gulp down air and plunging back down, back to the line of bubbles, guiding him to the bank.

With a bump, his shoulder hit land and he let himself flop over onto the gravelly beach. Between gasps of air, river water lurched out from his gut and onto the shore. The pain announced its return, seemingly everywhere at once. He couldn't bear it. Something washed up beside him, insisting at his leg.

The fedora hat.

If his arms had worked, he would have gladly flung it back out for the currents to bear away. Heat suddenly, on his cheek. A tear trickling over his graze.

The salty sting.

Yes.

He was beaten and beached, but at the least alive.

# 29

# FOR NOW

There were some weird and whacky dreams. When Ocean's blurry eyes parted, a man in a white pinafore stood at the end of the bed consulting a clipboard. He was going bald with scruffy facial hair and glasses.

'Am I alright?' His voice didn't sound like his own. It fell out in a weak, dry mumble.

The man glanced up. 'Ah, excellent, you're awake. I'm Dr Georgi. As for "being alright?" Well let's see here, I don't want to miss anything out.' He consulted the clipboard.

'Fractured kneecap; two broken fingers, three fractured fingers; two broken arms—one a double break; one dislocated shoulder; four cracked ribs; glass lacerations to the feet; two black eyes; severe grazing; concussion. In short, Mr Daley, no, you're not all right. But you're alive and extremely lucky to be in such a condition.'

'I don't feel very lucky.' Truth was, he'd been beat up worse than Rocky Balboa and had never felt physically or emotionally worse in his entire life.

'You don't look lucky either, but there you are.'

'So I really need all this?' Ocean nudged his head towards the stirrups his plastered arms were in and the thick bandaging around his knee.

The doctor raised an eyebrow. 'You think we'd wrap you up like an Egyptian Mummy for the fun of it? It'd give the nurses a giggle I expect.' He took a step towards the bed, cocked his head and squinted at Ocean's arm. 'We had to operate on your right arm to reset the bones. How's the pain?'

'Like normal pain. Just tons worse.'

The doctor grimaced. 'Yes, I'm sorry about that. I reduced the dosage. MI5 are here to talk to you and they want you cogent. I'll up it again once they're gone.'

'MI5?' He knew someone would come, but he'd assumed it would be the police. But then, why would it be? He'd been involved in an assassination attempt. A bomb had exploded in Wimbledon. He had tumbled from the top of Tower Bridge with the leader of a terrorist organisation into the Thames. No, a plain Bobby off the street wasn't going to cut the mustard.

The doctor scribbled a note, clicked the pen and slipped it into his top pocket. 'Speak to them now, I would. Then they'll finally let your poor mother in. She's been waiting outside for almost two days now.'

'Two *days*?'

But Dr Georgi was already beckoning them in. The MI5 agents were both in sleek black suits. The lead agent flashed an ID, then a smile.

'Ocean? I'm glad you're awake,' she pulled up a chair next to his bed. 'I'm Eva Langton, MI5. This is my colleague Davis Matthews. We need to ask you some questions.'

He met her green cat-like eyes. 'Why couldn't you let Mum in to see me?'

'Medical personnel only until we interview you. We've had a security detail on your door day and night and kept your identity out of the press. It is a matter of national security that we speak with you first.'

Matthews leant forward. 'We know about Orca. As long as they think you still haven't talked, your life is in immediate danger.'

'Orca will want to get me anyway whether I talk or not. What's left of Orca anyway.'

The agents exchanged a glance. 'You can confirm then, that Frank Daley fell with you?'

He nodded. 'Have you found his body?'

Matthews shook his head. 'Not yet. We're still searching.'

Langton took out a phone. 'Ocean, I need to record our conversation.'

He winced at the sight of it, remembering Slater. Did she have to use *that*? He stared at her insincere hand resting on his cast, his ridiculous gown and his bandages and sighed. He knew they had a job to do, but he wished these people would just go. He needed to see his mother.

'The quicker you start talking, the sooner we're out of here.' Langton said, sensing his mood.

He stared at the ceiling and wondered how to even begin.

It was like being too deep underwater, when the pressure pounds your ears and threatens to make your head pop. But once he started talking, it was like floating up into shallower water, the awful weight of it all eased with each millimetre he rose toward the surface. Those two hours of talking and cross-examination took him so far. But shame and guilt aren't feelings so easily dissolved.

Matthews shook his head in wonder at his pages of scribbled notes. Langton lifted a cup of water, and eased the straw to Ocean's lips: the talking had turned his already dry throat into desert.

'Will I be charged?' he asked once the cup was down.

Langton hesitated, threw a glance at her companion. 'There's something we'd like to offer you Ocean. An opportunity.'

'I've watched my share of cop shows. A plea bargain type thing?'

She sent him a smile. 'Not exactly. More, a working relationship—once you're fully recovered of course. Taking into account your somewhat foolish bravery and actions to save lives, we shan't be bringing any charges against you. We'll provide protection for your family ... but, we are counting on your assistance, just like you've helped us today,' she tapped the phone.

He was suddenly overwhelmed with tiredness. He couldn't think about all this now. 'I just want to see Mum.'

Matthews stood, straightened his suit. 'Sure. You've been through a lot, but think on it. We'll be in touch soon. We'll have plenty of follow-up from this initial interview. We'd like to find...' He checked something in his book, 'this Kaya, Claude and Dante. We already have one Drew Anderson in for questioning. I tell you, with your two broken arms, his two broken legs, it's a wonder we could make a complete human being out of the two of you.'

'But for now, you just keep mending.' Langton said. 'And remember. MI5 always needs special people like you.'

'Ha!' He scoffed, with a shake of his head. Frank's words were still fresh in his ears, all about his stupidity, his arrogance, believing the whole time he was special when it reality he'd been as easy to dupe as a toddler.

'That seem funny to you Ocean?'

'No. You've just got me all wrong. I'm not special.'

Agent Langton pushed her mouth to one side. 'Do you know what the kill rate is from a water landing at that height?'

'No.'

'Over 99%.'

He could only gape like a fool.

'See,' she smiled, 'you're more special that you realise.'

The agents had barely made it out the door before Mum came in, followed closely by a nurse who made a beeline for the drip.

'Ocean honey, look at the state of you.' Mum's eyes glistened in the stark hospital lights. She took a tentative step towards him. Another. Then gently, she eased past his casts and hugged him. Her hair smelt freshly washed, homely and clean and he realised, all in a rush, how much he had missed her, needed her and how terribly he had let her down.

'I'm so sorry.' He croaked into her neck knowing how insufficient a word it was when stacked alongside the deceitfulness that had nearly got them all killed.

'Shhh, don't. It's me, I should never have let you go.'

It was just like her to blame herself, to be so pure and good, trying to ease his burden of guilt.

'I'll never do anything like that again, I promise.'

'I know honey.'

And they held one another, or rather, she held him. When she drew apart, they looked at one another's teary eyes and burst into laughter. Ocean cut short with a wince.

'Don't make me laugh. My ribs aren't up to it yet.'

She took out a hankie, wiped her eyes and did the same for him. 'I'll do my best. Crabby.' She raised her pincers, but didn't use them.

'Mum,' he said, 'I can't wait to come home.'

After a week in hospital, Ocean returned home to Shoreham. It was a funny feeling, stepping into the terraced house again after more than two months away. It smelt uniquely of home, he could have recognised it blindfolded; the plain scent of their sun-baked carpet and Mum's potpourri bowl on the telephone table by the door. But whilst it looked and smelt the same, it felt different. It was a knocked slightly askew version of home, like a Hollywood set designer had made a perfect recreation of it just from photographs. But it wasn't the house that had changed, he knew.

Recovery was frustratingly slow. In his casts he had all the dexterity of a wooden coat hanger, but he could move the fingers on his left hand. And it was this ability that allowed him to conduct simple navigations on the iPad and leave a post on the Cádiz football club message board for Dante. Soon, his friend had set up a secure chat room and the two caught up on what had happened after they'd split. Dante reported how he'd managed to get a fake passport made and catch a series of trains back to Spain. He was now lying low in a remote mountain village in the Alpujarras, and Claude was apparently hiding out somewhere in Belgium.

Then it was Ocean's turn. Typing was painfully slow, but he managed to recount it all to his friend. The chase. Drew. Tower Bridge and the Thames.

'*Tío,*' Dante wrote, 'you're a true hero.'

It wasn't for modesty's sake that Ocean replied that no, he wasn't anything close to that. He was a screw up who'd gotten extremely lucky. He'd almost got his Mum killed, not to mention himself.

'For me, *tío*, you are a true hero. Whatever you say. And you know something else?'

'What?'

'If you'd told me you had two broken arms we would have Skyped instead!'

MI5 had discreetly invested in CCTV cameras to monitor activity across Shoreham beach. There were agents stationed in shifts opposite the house, posing as kite surfers in an old VW. An attack team was targeting the remaining known members of Orca, the Holborn safe house and Hinckley Farm.

Ocean doubted they'd find anyone. He wondered how Orca would react. Scarlet was the most likely to take over. That was a scary thought, not least because she had just lost Frank. For now, he had to hope MI5 were up to keeping them safe while he recovered. In this convalescence, Ocean found that time operated in super slow-mo. It was monotonous. Whenever he wasn't chatting to Dante he was watching TV. He got up to season five in *Breaking Bad,* watched the *Tour de France*, the Grand Prix (including qualifying) and pretty much every ball of the Ashes. It was better than nothing, but only just. He longed to be playing sports again: to go swimming, play tennis and basketball. But this, he told himself was his penance. It was what he owed the cosmos for his mistakes and the unit of the debt was time, with unrelenting boredom charged as the commission.

There were positives. He was getting on well with Andy, even going to site with the Lightning Crew one day just for a change of scene. Andy, he realised was a good person deep down, even if he was still a bit disgusting. Mum had asked

Ocean if he would give her away at their wedding and he was only too glad to accept. As far as he was concerned, he owed them both all he could give.

Some days he would go to the beach and wade into the sea up to the knees, an agent always lingering behind on the beach. The water was so blue and crystal clear some days; it was like a taunt to not to be able to dive all the way in.

By the end of August, his ribs were better, his left arm out of its cast and he felt like he could start jogging soon. By then he was so bored of being in the house that he was even looking forward to going back to school, something he would have found inconceivable a few months ago.

In early September, a little before the start of term, he sat on the stones watching the windsurfers skip and tear across the sea. He caught glimpses of the yellow buoy by the shipping lane. He would never be able to look at that thing without thinking of Dad. But that was okay. It was better than some mossy tombstone. He could look at that buoy and feel good, safe even. All the complexity and confusion he'd felt towards Dad wasn't there anymore. There was just peace.

Stones crunched behind him. He turned. Agents Langton and Matthews were approaching. About time.

'Let me guess. Still not found his body?' Ocean called.

Langton pushed up her sunglasses into her hair to stop it from flailing around in the wind. 'Doubt we will.'

A 99% kill rate from that height, the agent had said. And Ocean was a born swimmer, young and resilient ...

'Got some good news though.' Matthews tossed him a newspaper. 'Looks like the delayed vote went the right way. Lord Cloudsley's written a good piece on it on page four if you're interested.'

'They're not selling the weapons then ...' Ocean smoothed the paper in his free hand. Well that was something wasn't it? Some good to come from all this. 'Can I keep it to read later?'

'Sure.' Matthews said.

Langton crouched down and gently examined the side of his face with a fingertip, tracing a line around the ghost of his cheek graze.

'You're healing well. Your Mum tells me you should be completely back to normal in a few months.'

'Yeah, whatever normal is.' Ocean nudged some of the stones with his foot. 'But I'm on the mend, thanks.'

'Have you thought about our offer?'

He hadn't really, despite all the time on his hands. He shook his head and stared back out to sea.

'You know, we actually used to work with your father. Before Frank took over and radicalised it, Orca were an ally, a force for good.' Langton said. 'But now they've slipped up. For the first time we've got a chance to neutralise them, to save thousands of lives. And for that, we could really use your help. You actually know these people. You've spent time with them. To us they're just ghosts.'

It was in his own interest too, he knew, but he didn't have the strength. Not yet.

There were starlings on the horizon flying in a flock, turning, shape-shifting in the wind like a bitty black wave over the foamy sea.

'I'm happy just to be back here, at home, in Shoreham for now.'

He waited a beat and nodded his head.

'Just for now.'

# AUTHOR'S NOTE

Thank you for reading Orca Rising, I hope you enjoyed reading it as much as I did writing it.

Nearly 90% of people check reviews when deciding their next book purchase. If you enjoyed Orca Rising, you can keep me writing by leaving an honest review. It'll also help other readers with tastes like you find a path to my book.

If you're thirsty for more, join fans of the Orca series in my reader's club for updates, giveaways and more: visit csjhannon.com to sign up.

Ocean is back in action, in the follow-up: **Orca Rogue Agent**
**Read on for Chapter 1...**

# ORCA ROGUE AGENT

## 1

## ZURBARÁN

'**H**e's a master of surprise and reinvention. One moment you think you understand him, the next...' Ms Martínez flicked out her fingers and made the sound of an explosion, like her mind was blown.

Fifteen students from Shoreham Academy were gathered in the lobby of London's Tate Museum, all trying to follow the ethereal Ms Martínez. Ocean Daley hung at the back with his friends Sam and Alicia.

'What? You spontaneously combust?' he murmured.

Sam covered his laugh with a clipboard. Alicia grinned.

'Picasso's genius just...' Ms Martinez trailed off again and tipped her face to the ceiling as if the painter was looking down on her from heaven. She quickly made the sign of the cross to gather her wits. 'But it's not all about Picasso, this is a journey through the history of the great Spanish painters, from El Greco to the seventeenth century *Sevillano* masters Velázquez, Zurbarán and Murillo right through to Miró, Picasso and Dalí. A treat of the senses, to understand, to taste the Spanish blood!' She'd lost them all now.

Ocean had to wonder exactly how this Spanish day was going to help them with their Spanish A-Levels. In lieu of a fallen through exchange trip –which might have actually helped their speaking and listening– Ms Martínez had organised a museum trip to gawk at some paintings followed by a late lunch at a tapas bar. No doubt their learning would be completed by a siesta on the coach back home that very afternoon.

Armed with language worksheets, the students broke away into smaller groups. The first room in the gallery had three exits. Two security guards sat at either end of the room; one was armed with a right-handed holster. The second had a baton, also right-handed. Ocean closed his eyes and tested himself, doing a roll call of the civilians in the room; rough age, height, any detail he could remember. He opened them, checked his count. Twelve civilians, details on the money. These assessments were good protocol sure, but more than that: he was suspicious of everybody.

Orca, the spy organisation –no, the terrorists he'd unwittingly joined– were still out there. They were dangerous and still smarting from the death of Frank, his uncle and their leader. And they blamed Ocean for it.

'Hey, check this out.' Alicia and Sam each grabbed an arm, pulling him from his thoughts and into an alcove. Here, there was an actor dressed up like a painter, Picasso he guessed, daubing paint onto a canvas, occasionally looking up into the middle distance as if channelling inspiration.

'Great,' Ocean said, nonplussed.

'You know it's a hologram, right?' Sam asked.

'A hologram?'

'Says so right there,' said Alicia, pointing at an information plaque on the side.

Ocean squinted at Picasso, not quite able to believe it. The colours were...what? Firm. Solid somehow. Hard light?

'No way,' he reached for it, fingers tingling. Would they pass straight through or meet solid–

'Oi, no touching.' A security guard said wearily.

'You probably say that about a gazillion times a day.' Alicia said sympathetically. 'It must be annoying when people can't just read the massive *Don't Touch* sign above it, hey Ocean?' she wore a wicked grin. 'Remind me how many A-Levels you're doing again? Six was it? Double what us mere mortals do, and yet you clearly have no common sense.'

'Five actually, you can't count General Studies. And if it really is a hologram then it's made of light, so I don't see why touching it is a problem, it's not like I'm going to leave my fingerprints on it.'

'Smartass.' Alicia mumbled.

Ocean got permission from the guard to take a few shots of the hologram on his phone. He opened a secure app, one his friend Dante –a tech genius– had designed for encrypted contact. There were three of them in the chat: Dante, Claude and himself, all survivors from the Orca program.

The chat was named 'Orca Exiles' and for its icon Dante had chosen an image from some 90s film called *Free Willy*. Ocean had never seen or even heard of the film but the icon was perfect. It showed a killer whale leaping to its escape over an aquarium wall, arcing over a boy's hand towards the sea. Dante's attempts at humour often misfired, so for him, this was actually pretty good.

Ocean picked the best shot of Picasso and captioned the picture: O: Check this hologram out! Most amazing tech I've ever seen! This'll put Madame Tussauds out of business.

Ocean smiled to himself, now *that* was funny. The next room was full of religious paintings. Lots depicted the crucifixion of Christ, one by a guy called Zurbarán caught his eye. It was painted with photo-like realism on a dark background, so life-like it was almost beyond real. In its way, it was beautiful.

'God isn't this boring?' Alicia poked Ocean playfully in the ribs.

'Hey!' he laughed, slapping her arm away. Alicia had a knowing grin and covetous eyes. He felt a warmth come to his cheeks and stared at his trainers.

Alicia leaned over. 'Don't worry Ocean, I like them shy.'

Sam cleared his throat and in slightly too loud a voice said: 'Here it says that back in the day, people were sceptical that there could be a Virgin Mother.'

'Well, duh.' Alicia said.

'So, basically they painted a bunch of Virgin Marys with babies as if that would prove that it did happen. So maybe if I paint a picture of myself playing in the NBA then that'd make it true!' Sam waited for a laugh from Alicia that didn't come. His disappointment was badly disguised. Sam looked pleadingly to Ocean, but what could he do about it? Ocean turned away from them both and faced a colourful Picasso depicting three pyramids. Perfect triangles.

'I want to ask Ms Martínez something, you two go on ahead into the next room. I'll catch up.' Ocean didn't wait for a reply and pretended to look for their teacher.

His phone buzzed in his pocket. Replies from Claude and Dante. But what was this? Unbelievable. They hadn't got the Madame Tussauds reference. Maybe Sam wasn't the only one who's jokes sucked. Dante wasn't even that impressed with the hologram either.

D: '*Tío*, that tech's been available for years. In ten years, today's TV screens won't exist except in old people's homes. It'll be holographic 3D TV you watch on your coffee table. The big corps are just holding it back to milk every Euro they can out of the HD/OLED market.'

Bloody know it all. Ocean stuffed the phone back into his pocket. No sign of Ms Martínez but he was at least in a different room to Sam, Alicia and awkwardville. From behind him, a metallic sound dented the low museum hush. Suddenly alert, Ocean turned, searching for the location of the metallic rattling sound until there it was, rolling across the floor to a stop. A thermos flask.

Then each end of the thermos flicked open and thick white smoke billowed out of both ends.

'Everyone, get out!' he yelled, pulling his jumper over his mouth. One of the security guards hit an alarm by the wall and drew his gun.

'Holster that gun!' Ocean shouted. The room disappeared into thick white cloud. Ocean sniffed. It didn't smell like gas. Screams. Footsteps. Confusion.

So, this was it then. Orca had finally come him.

*** 

*Read on: Orca Rogue Agent is available on ebook and paperback.*

# CONNECT WITH THE AUTHOR

Join fans of the Orca series on my list for updates, giveaways and more at my website **csjhannon.com**

**Follow me on:**
Twitter **@csjhannon**
Bookbub **@csjhannon**
Goodreads – **Chris Hannon**
Instagram-**@csjhannon1**

# OTHER BOOKS BY THE AUTHOR

## Young Adult

Perry Scrimshaw's Rite of Passage (2015)

### *Orca series*
Orca Rising (2018)
Orca Rouge Agent (2019)
Orca Divinity Fix (2021)

## Adult
Dark Vet (2021)

Manufactured by Amazon.ca
Bolton, ON